WHERE WE LIVE AND DIE

Stories about Writing

BRIAN KEENE

LAZY FASCIST PRESS

LAZY FASCIST PRESS
P.O. BOX 10065
PORTLAND, OR 97296

www.lazyfascistpress.com

ISBN: 978-1-62105-191-6

"Writing About Writing: An Introduction" is original to this collection.
"The Girl on the Glider" first published as *The Girl on the Glider*, Cemetery Dance, 2010.
"Musings" first published in *4 Killers*, Cemetery Dance, 2013.
"Golden Boy" first published in *The Little Silver Book of Streetwise Stories*, Borderlands Press, 2008.
"The Eleventh Muse" first published in *Carpe Noctem*, 2015.
"The House of Ushers" first published in *Infernally Yours*, Necro Publications, 2009.
"The Revolution Happened While You Were Sleeping (A Summoning Spell) – Remixed" is original to this collection. An alternate audio version first appeared on *Talking Smack*, Medium Rare Books, 2002.
"Things They Don't Teach You In Writing Class" first published in *Trigger Warnings*, 2015.
"Notes About Writing About Writing" is original to this collection.

Printed in the USA.

TABLE OF CONTENTS

ACKNOWLEDGMENTS

Thanks to Cameron Pierce, Jeff Burk, and everyone else at Lazy Fascist, Deadite, and Eraserhead; the editors who originally published these works in other forms; and my sons.

This one is for John Skipp and Alan M. Clark…

WHERE WE LIVE AND DIE

Stories about Writing

"All houses wherein men have lived and died
Are haunted houses."

—Henry Wadsworth Longfellow, *Haunted Houses*

Writing About Writing:
An Introduction

The number one bit of advice given to all would-be writers is to "write what you know." This line of wisdom can be interpreted in many different ways. Maybe you recently suffered a terrible heartbreak—the end of a romantic relationship or the loss of a loved one. The emotions stemming from something so painful can be mined for fiction, i.e. writing what you know. The flip side is also true. Maybe you just fell in love or held a sleeping baby. The joy those situations bring can also be used in fiction. Writing what you know can also involve your circumstances, situation, or station in life. When I first started writing with professional publication in mind, most of my characters were blue-collar young males stuck in dead end factory jobs in dead end towns. That's because I was writing what I knew. I was a blue-collar young male stuck in a series of dead end factory jobs in a dead end town.

This is why, eventually, every writer of literary or popular fiction inevitably ends up writing about writing at some point in their career. It doesn't matter what genre, or what style. Horror, bizarro, romance, mystery, thriller, science-fiction, graphic novels...even those seemingly plotless bestselling literary darlings that eschew genre classification and used to get cooed about on Oprah. Read enough of them, and you'll encounter a story about a writer.

That's because the writers are writing about what they know. They're writing about writing, and what it is to be a writer.

I've done the same thing a few times in my career. In the novels *Dark Hollow* and *The Complex*, the novella *Sundancing*, and in the stories collected in this book. And because my muse tends to lean toward things horrific and bizarre, it should come as no surprise that the elements of writing for a living I've chronicled over the years are equally horrific and bizarre. All of these stories are about writing, and all of them fall under either the horror or bizarro genre labels. Two of them—"The Girl on the Glider" and "Musings"—are meta-fiction, in which I, the writer, become a character in the tale—which is just an even deeper level of writing what you know.

This collection's origins were sort of a happy accident. Cameron Pierce of Lazy Fascist approached me about reprinting "The Girl on the Glider" in paperback. I was hesitant about that idea for a couple reasons. First of all, it had been published in hardcover, and was also available in a paperback short story collection as well as in various digital platforms (Kindle, Nook, Kobo, etc.). I felt it would be unfair to readers to release it as a stand-alone paperback when they could already get it elsewhere. Secondly, while the story's length is fine for a collectible hardcover, it would have made for a slim paperback volume. So, I emailed Cameron back and politely declined. But Cameron, persistent and two-fisted editor that he is, then threw a Henry Wadsworth Longfellow quote at me (the same quote that is used as this book's epigraph) and asked, "What if we collected all of your stories about writing, instead?"

And so we did.

Enjoy!

Brian Keene
May 2015

THE GIRL ON THE GLIDER

"Very nearly all the ghost stories of old times claim to be true narratives of remarkable occurrences."
—M. R. James, *Some Remarks on Ghost Stories*

"Everything dies, but not everything has an ending."
—Brian Keene, *City of the Dead*

"Chugga chugga, choo choo, spin around. Every letter has a sound…"
—Children's Toy

ENTRY 1:

I dreamed about her again last night—the girl on the glider. Apparently, I was kicking and thrashing so hard in my sleep that I woke up my wife. She wasn't very happy about it, either. The baby has been getting up between 4am and 5am every morning, and Cassi didn't appreciate me waking her a few hours before that.

This morning, while we were giving the baby his breakfast, Cassi asked me if I remembered what I was dreaming about. I lied and told her that I didn't.

Anyway, it's clear that this shit isn't going away on its own. If anything, it's getting worse. I'm not one-hundred percent positive that I know who the girl is, or why she's hanging out on our porch glider, or why I'm dreaming about her, but I have some ideas. The only problem is that my ideas all point to one solution. One answer.

And the answer is that I'm losing my fucking mind.

That scares me. That scares me in ways I can't even put into words (which is frustrating for a writer). I mean, at forty-one—or am I forty-two? I can't remember. Isn't it funny how you stop keeping track of that shit after a certain age? Let's see. Dad came back from Vietnam in 1967 and I came along nine months later, so that makes me...forty-one. I think. Math was never my strong suit. Let's say, for the sake of argument, that I'm forty-one, which sucks, but doesn't suck nearly as bad as being forty-two.

But I digress, new diary. As I was saying, at forty-one, I've thought about my own mortality a little bit. I don't like to, but I really don't have any choice, do I? After my Dad's cancer battle and the fact that I'm a father again—it makes a guy think long and hard about things. I've led a pretty hardcore lifestyle. That shit takes a toll on you after a while. Sooner or later, it catches up with you.

In truth, I always figured it would be my past that killed me—the booze or the tobacco or the era of loose sex all seemed to be likely candidates. Or maybe a slick road combined with a high rate of speed and some heavy metal blasting from the speakers. Or maybe I'd go out like

Dick Laymon and my Grandma Lena did—a quick and sudden heart attack. Or maybe I'd get gunned down at a book signing by some crazed fan. "Here ya go, zombie guy! Let's see you come back from the dead!"

Click click, bang. Curtains close, and…scene. Type 'The End.'

None of those would be pleasant. Especially cancer. I'm scared to fucking death of cancer. I can't think of anything more horrifying than dying of cancer. I'd rather drown or burn to death than die of cancer. But losing my mind terrifies me even more than cancer does, because if I lost my mind, I wouldn't be able to write anymore. Losing my voice wouldn't impact my writing. Neither would losing my legs or my sight or my hearing. Even if I lost my hands, I'd still be able to write. There's voice recognition software and other methods I could use. The only part of my body I couldn't write without is my brain, and apparently, my brain has decided to declare war on me.

That's why I've started writing this manuscript. Diary. Whatever the fuck it is. I'm writing it to help me work out this shit on my own. I mean, let's be realistic. It's not like I can Blog about it. They make fun of Whitley Strieber for saying he was abducted by grey aliens possessed with a disturbing fascination for his bunghole. Imagine what they'd do to me if I said in public that I was being haunted by a teenaged girl who likes to hang out on my porch and send text messages on her cell phone and talk to my nineteen-month-old son and occasionally scare the shit out of my dog—even if she's not probing my ass the way Whitley's aliens do.

I can't talk about it online, and I can't tell my friends

about it, either. It's hard times right now, especially for writers. Tough financial straits. You'd think that people would buy more books during a recession, but apparently, it's quite the opposite. J. F. (Jesus) Gonzalez and Tim Lebbon and Tom Piccirilli and Jim Moore and everybody else I know are in the same financial situation that I'm in, and I don't foresee the President or Congress giving us a corporate bailout anytime soon. My peers have problems of their own. They've got enough on their minds. They don't need one of their best writer-friends confiding in them that he might very well be going crazy. And if I told my inner circle—John Urbancik, Geoff "Coop" Cooper, Mike Oliveri and Michael "Mikey" Huyck—I'm pretty sure they would try to set up some kind of intervention for me, and who needs that shit, right? I'm still pissed about the last time they tried to do that to me.

I could tell Cassi, I guess. I mean, she's my wife. I'm supposed to tell her everything, but for some reason, I haven't told her about this. To be honest, I think she already suspects. She's commented a few times over the last couple of weeks that I seem out of it. And she's right. I am a bit out of it. But I can't tell her everything yet, because I don't want to scare her. If I start crying or something—if I break down—it will really frighten her, and right now, with everything else that's going on, I have to be the strong one. For her. The baby. Our friends and families. All of us.

So I'm telling you.

Dear new manuscript that I'm typing on my laptop:

My name is Brian Keene and I am either losing my mind or I am being haunted.

Or both.

That's a start. Feels good to type it, though. This can be like my own little private blog. I'll break the entries up into chapters. Maybe include a few footnotes. It will feel just like any other manuscript. Maybe then I can get at the truth. We'll call it meta-fiction or gonzo—the blending of fact and fiction, the inserting of the author into the narrative. If it's good enough for Hunter S. Thompson and Tim Powers and Stephen King (who inserted himself as a character into the *Dark Tower* series) then I reckon it's good enough for me, too.

More tomorrow. Got up at 5:30am this morning. It's now 11:07pm and I'm frigging exhausted. Been working on that novella for Cemetery Dance all day (the weird western novella that I still don't have a working title for— I'm considering calling it *An Occurrence in Crazy Bear Valley*). Joe Lansdale, who is the man I'd most like to be when I grow up, once told me that he writes two to four hours a day. That's what I aspire to. That's what I hope I'm doing when I'm his age. But I'm not. And to pay the bills, I put in long hours at the keyboard every fucking day, writing about zombies and ghouls and satyrs and giant carnivorous worms. Anyway, my point is that I'm tired (you can tell, because I have a tendency to ramble when I'm tired). I'm gonna finish this cigar, have a glass of Basil Hayden's while I walk the dog, and then I'm going to bed.

Hopefully, I won't dream about her tonight.

ENTRY 2:

No dreams last night, at least, none that I remember. Cassi didn't mention that I'd woke her up by having nightmares either. There was one weird thing last night, though. I'd gone to bed after typing that first entry, and I was just starting to drift off—in that weird state where I wasn't quite asleep but not quite fully awake either—and then I heard an electronic beeping noise, like somebody was typing a text message on a cell phone. It was coming from the bathroom that's adjacent to our bedroom. Do you know what's on the other side of that bathroom wall?

The outside of our house. Specifically, our deck and the porch glider.

I'd like to think it was my imagination. I'd like to chalk it up to the fact that I've been thinking about all the weird shit too much, and now I'm starting to conjure up strangeness myself when nothing else is happening.

Except that this wasn't the first time I've heard it.

Okay, back to work. Finished this week's free internet serial installment of *Earthworm Gods II: Deluge* but need to spend the rest of the night working on this frigging Bigfoot novella. Damn thing is kicking my ass, which pisses me off, because otherwise, it's been a lot of fun to write.

ENTRY 3:

It's been a while since I worked on this. Ended up buried in deadlines—finishing the Bigfoot story and working on *A Gathering of Crows*, a Superman Halloween story script for DC comics, and a bunch of other stuff. Some of it will bring us money, which is good because we could really use it right now. The economy has gotten worse and the apocalypse is now upon us, at least as far as the small press goes. Once-reliable publishers are now either late with the royalty payments or simply ducking my calls and emails (and the calls and emails from others whom they owe). Thank God or Cthulhu that my mass-market checks are still arriving on time and that I've got comic book work and my temporary gig as an adjunct professor at York College to round out my income, because I suspect the days of the mid-list, working writer are coming to a close. We are a dying breed.

Dying. Death. Christ, I'm a cheery little fucker, huh? That's me. I'm Mr. Sunshine. I'm all about shiny happy people holding fucking hands and singing "Kumbaya."

It's not lost on me that I seem preoccupied with death and dying lately. I don't know why. Like I said earlier, maybe it's because of all the recent health scares in my family. But we've had health scares before and they didn't impact me this way. I don't know. I have to wonder if this is some sort of mid-life crisis type of mind-fuck. Certainly, I'm no stranger to death. I've known people who died. One set of grandparents, my great-uncle Hobie, several extended family members, Navy buddies, friends from high school, homeys from my days living on the streets, co-workers, Dick Laymon.

The three babies Cassi and I lost…

But I wrote about the babies already. I've been known to tell reporters that "writing is cheaper than therapy" and I always grin when I say it, to show that I'm just joking around, but the fact is I'm not fucking joking. Let me tell you something. There are many reasons why I identify with the fictional character of Tony Soprano—enough that I could write an entire book about it. One of the reasons is we have similar views on therapy. I've been to therapy, and therapy is bullshit. Yes, it works for other people, and I'm not belittling its overall value—but I'm telling you that it doesn't work for me. What works for me is to write about what's on my mind. Write about the shit going on in my life. *Dark Hollow* was me writing about me and Cassi's loss. Readers don't know that, but I do. Readers think it was just a fun little book about a satyr in suburbia, but I know that chapter two was the closest fucking thing to an autobiography I've ever written. Hell, the whole book was autobiographical. Adam Senft = Brian Keene. His doubts about his manhood and feelings of inadequacy because of his inability to save his loved ones was something I was intimately familiar with at the time. It was a hard novel to write. No, wait. Scratch that. It was an emotionally harrowing and utterly brutalizing novel to write. I went to a very dark place for that book, and I didn't come out again until I'd dredged up everything and vomited it out onto the page and bared my soul and almost killed myself in the process. Writing books like that one—pouring your personal shit into a novel or a short story—that's like confession and an exorcism and six months of therapy all rolled into one. I don't need Prozac or Lithium. I have a laptop and a publishing contract.

Shit. Now I'm rambling again. My point is this: I'm no stranger to death. We're old friends, he and I. At the very least, we're acquaintances. We recognize each other at the party and perhaps we nod in passing. I've watched people die. I've held them in my arms and had my hands turn sticky from their blood and felt the warmth drain out of them.

So why is it bothering me now? Why, after all this time, am I dwelling on it?

Anyway, enough about that.

My son, who is nineteen months old, looks at the top of our driveway and waves to somebody who isn't there. He always greets them with "Hi." Then he smiles. Occasionally, he giggles—the same little laugh he does when Cassi and I make faces at him. When I turn to look at who he's talking to, the driveway is empty.

I am not crazy.

ENTRY 4:

I guess I should start at the beginning. That's the only way I'll make any sense of this. I went back and re-read the previous entries again tonight, after I was finished looking for a short story I could let Stephen Jones reprint for an anthology he's putting together, and what I've written so far is nothing more than the incoherent, self-indulgent babblings of a madman. That won't do, especially since I'm trying to prove to myself that I'm not insane.

So...

In the beginning, I started making enough money as a writer that my wife and I were able to move out of our small home on Main Street in Shrewsbury, and buy a place out in the country instead. I like our home very much. It reminds me of the type of area I grew up in, and those kinds of places aren't very easy to find anymore. Everything is suburbs now—suburbs marking the distance between the next cluster of Home Depots and Walmarts and Burger Kings. Everything is sidewalks and homeowners' associations and McMansions and housing developments with names like Whispering Pines that don't have a single fucking pine tree, whispering or otherwise.

Our place isn't like that at all. It is distinctly old school. We have three acres of rural land. There are lots of tall, old-growth sycamore trees growing in our yard, and at the far end of our property, there is a swift, cold trout stream about twelve feet across and knee-deep in most places. In the spring, the creek often floods. We've got a neighbor on one side of our property. We share a driveway with him (the driveway is important and we'll come back to it in a minute). The other side of our property borders a vast marsh. Beyond the swamp is four miles of state-owned game land—a lush, thick wilderness that, by law, can never be developed or forested. Beyond these woods lies the Susquehanna River, which our trout stream also feeds into. There's an old logging road that runs from the edge of our property and through the woods, all the way to the river. Once, when Tim Lebbon was visiting, I took him for a walk back through there. He proclaimed it one of the most beautiful places on earth.

And it is.

A brief aside. I just cheated. It's late and I want to shut this laptop off and go to sleep, so I took a shortcut. I copied and pasted the description of the house from my novella *Scratch* into this document, and then changed the tense and a few other things. That's because the house in *Scratch* is this house, and their landscapes are the same. Both are beautiful, and I love this place as much as the character of Evan in *Scratch* loved his. That's why it concerns me that Cassi has recently floated the idea of buying a house somewhere else. I'm not sure what has prompted this desire. It makes no sense, certainly not in this economy. I have to wonder if she's seeing some of the same things I've been seeing. I know that in at least one case, she has, but I wonder if there's more. Perhaps she's keeping secrets from me, just as I'm keeping them from her. Maybe she's seen and heard more than she's letting on. Maybe I'm not crazy. Or maybe she's just as crazy as I am.

Anyway…the driveway. The driveway is an important part of this story, so let's talk about that. As I said before, it's a shared driveway, meaning me and Cassi and our neighbor and his wife all use it. It's all uphill, and a real bitch to shovel in the winter. It empties out onto a winding, two-lane back road that is frequented all day and night by speeding dump trucks, speeding tractor trailers, speeding teenagers, and speeding commuters trying to find a shortcut on their way to their jobs in Baltimore, Lancaster, Harrisburg and York. The posted speed limit is forty-five miles per hour, but I've never seen anybody go slower than sixty-five. Since we're right on the township line, we're not an ideal area for speed traps. By the time a cop on our side of the line pulled out in pursuit of a speeding car, the violator would already be in the next township.

We've lived here five years, and in that time there have been over twenty serious accidents (that I know of) within two miles of our driveway, plus countless fender-benders and other vehicular mishaps. Indeed, our first winter at the house, an ice storm turned York County's roads into Slip 'n Slides and our road was wall-to-wall fender-benders that morning. Automobiles were smashing into each other like bumper cars and lining up in front of our house. I stood out there and directed traffic and brought folks coffee until the fire department arrived.

I know of four fatalities that have occurred in the time we've lived here. I personally witnessed one of them. A couple on a motorcycle rear-ended a pick-up truck that was making a left turn. Both riders were ejected from the bike. The woman's head cracked like an egg inside her helmet. There wasn't much the truck driver, my neighbor, or myself could do for her. She was dead before the paramedics arrived. I never found out what happened to the guy that was on the bike with her, but I remember that his chest looked like raw hamburger.

One of the other fatalities happened about a mile from our house. A machine operator from the Harley Davidson plant was coming home after second shift and hit a tree. The tree won. Speculation is that the driver fell asleep at the wheel. The third fatal accident happened fifty yards from our driveway. A lone driver ran down an embankment at three in the morning. The accident was quiet enough that both my neighbors and my wife and I slept through it. We didn't know anything was amiss until we heard the sirens outside. By then it was too late, although, judging by the condition of the car and the body, it would have been too late long before they arrived.

The fourth fatality occurred at the top of our driveway.

And that was how I met the girl on the glider. And that is where our story really begins.

ENTRY 5:

I wasn't home when it happened. It was mid-January, and I was a Guest of Honor at a convention in Missouri called VisionCon. After Saturday's book signing and Q&A were over with, I spent the evening hanging out in the hotel bar with Mike Oliveri, Cullen Bunn, Val Botchlet (who used to moderate my old message board forum), my friend Richard Christy's cousin Adam, playwright Roy C. Booth, and the guys from Skullvines Press. I was pleased to note that the hotel bar, upon learning that I would be back in town that weekend, had Basil Hayden's and Knob Creek on hand (the year before, they'd only had Jack Daniel's and Jim Beam available, which are like the Coors and Budweiser of bourbon). Needless to say, we had a good time, and I didn't get to bed until after 3am.

When I woke up the next morning, I called home to talk to Cassi. She sounded tired and I soon found out why. She hadn't gotten much sleep the night before. She told me there had been another accident. Four kids, all of them between the ages of eighteen and twenty, had wrecked their car right at the top of our driveway. Three walked away from the accident. One did not. The accident happened just after midnight. Emergency vehicles, firemen and paramedics had been on hand until well after dawn. Had Cassi experienced some kind of crisis, and had to leave our home, she would have been unable to get out of our driveway. The emergency crews had it blocked off, along with the road. I asked her if she knew the details and found out that she didn't. All she knew was what one of the paramedics had told her—the wreck, the number and ages of the people in the car, and that one of them had died. I asked her if Coop had been on the scene, since he works as an EMT and our road is along his ambulance route. It turned out he hadn't. While all of this was going on, Coop and the rest of his ambulance crew had been down at the river, fishing a suicide out of the half-frozen water near the Columbia-Marietta Bridge.

My flight home from Missouri was delayed until Monday night due to inclement weather. I didn't land in Baltimore until nearly midnight and didn't get home until after 2am Tuesday morning. I didn't bother to look for damage from the accident or markings on the road. It was dark and foggy outside, and I was focused solely on giving my wife, my son and my dog all a big hug. I didn't see anything that night, supernatural or otherwise.

I wonder now, looking back, if I might have seen something then had I been looking for it—and if I had seen something, would I have known what it was?

The next morning, after I woke up and unpacked and told my wife about my trip, I remembered the accident and decided to walk up to the top of the driveway and survey the damage. Yes, I'm one of those people who slow down to gawk at accidents on the highway. I'll stand and watch a burning building. I'm fascinated by such things. To be fair, though, I'd like to think that I'm also the type of person who will stop along that highway and offer assistance, or run inside that burning building and pull people out until the firemen arrive. This is what I tell myself, at least.

I walked up the driveway and was out of breath by the time I reached the top. This happens a lot—more and more these last few years. When I was a kid, I could ride my BMX Mongoose all over York County, pedaling down to Spring Grove to buy comic books at the newsstand, and not get winded. In the Navy, I could swim a mile and not be out of breath. I used to run cross country in high school (the only organized sport I ever played, and I did it just to make my old man happy). But now, at forty-one? Forget about it. I gasp for breath after walking a mile through the woods and vigorous sex sometimes leaves me winded and on the verge of passing out. There are times when I lay there on the bed, wheezing and panting and waiting for the room to stop spinning. I told Cassi she should consider my breathlessness a compliment, but she doesn't see it that way. It concerned Cassi enough that she made me go to the doctor. I hate doctors. I could cut my arm off in a horrific threshing machine accident and I still wouldn't go to the doctor. But I went for her. The doctor said there wasn't anything wrong with me. No heart trouble (at least, not yet). No lung trouble. In plain terms, I was out of fucking shape. I asked him how this could be. He asked me what I did for a living. I told him I sat around in my underwear and made up scary stories all day long. He frowned, as if to say, "Well, there's your answer."

I was never the athletic type. Sure, I can hold my own in a fight (and I am mean enough to win), but I'm not much for playing sports or exercising or things like that. Under orders to get in shape, I went to the one person whose advice I trust in such a situation—Wrath James White, former World Champion kickboxer, UFC trainer and fighter, horror novelist, and one of my best friends. He told me to run every day. He said I should start out running, and when I felt like I couldn't go on, that instead of stopping, I should walk. Then, after a little bit of walking, I should start running again. Wrath told me to do this every day, and I'd be in shape in no time. I did it once and it almost killed me.

I'm certain this was Wrath's idea of a practical joke.

Anyway, I stood at the top of the driveway and looked

around while I caught my breath. It was easy to tell what had happened. The car had been coming north and heading southwest when, for whatever reason, the driver lost control. It had swerved up the embankment on the far side of the road, missing our mailbox by inches. Then it had flipped over onto its roof, slid back across the road, and slammed into the guardrail next to our driveway. There was debris and markings everywhere. The tires had gouged huge trenches in the embankment, and a piece of the muffler had come off on a chunk of granite sticking up out of the dirt. The pavement was scratched and scuffed, and covered with fragments of windshield glass and shards of plastic from the headlights, taillights and elsewhere. There were a bunch of other tiny parts. I don't know shit about cars, but I bet Coop could have identified them easily enough (Coop once took it upon himself to teach me how to fix a car. Within an hour, he'd grown annoyed enough to tell me that the timing belt ran the digital clock on my dashboard. I believed him. It was my wife who eventually set me straight).

Some of the junk was lying in our driveway. I'd probably driven right over it the night before. I wondered why the cops hadn't done a better job of cleaning up after the accident. Maybe it was because there were just so many crashes on this road, and they knew they'd have to do it all over again soon enough. There was more debris scattered around the crumpled guardrail, along with bent and broken saplings and vegetation.

There were black and brown stains on the road. The heaviest concentration of them seemed to be about ten feet away from the guardrail. The black stuff was oil.

The brown stains were blood. Around these, the State Police investigators had spray-painted arrows, circles and numbers. Number one corresponded with the embankment. Number four corresponded with the largest of the bloodstains. These modern day hieroglyphics told me a story. Someone had been ejected from the car when it flipped over onto its roof. That person was thrown further down the road while the car and the other three occupants slid toward the guardrail. I wondered who came to a stop first. I was pretty sure, judging by the visual evidence, that the person who'd been ejected was the one who had died.

I walked back down to the house, went out into the garage, and got a broom and a snow shovel. Then I trekked back up to the top of the hill and swept the debris out of our driveway. When I was finished, I went out to my office and settled in to do some work. Nothing relaxes me more than sitting in my office after I've been out on the road, and this was my first chance to enjoy it since coming home from VisionCon. I started writing, and didn't think about the accident again until the next day, when the cross showed up.

ENTRY 6:

The only newspaper I read is *USA Today*, and the only time I read it is when I'm traveling. I've tried twice to subscribe to it, but each time I was told that we lived too far out in the country for them to deliver it. We don't subscribe to either of the local papers. It's nothing personal. I have good friends at both the *York Daily Record* and the *York Dispatch*. Indeed, before I went full-time as a novelist, I used to supplement my income as a freelance writer for the

York Dispatch/York Sunday News. Both papers have given me reasonably fair coverage over the years (other than the time they mistakenly reported that I was quitting horror to write a Civil War novel). I have nothing against either publication, but I don't subscribe to either. I read the news online when I wake up in the morning. By the time the local paper would arrive, I'd already be working, so it doesn't make sense for me to subscribe.

Both papers had, in fact, reported on the accident, but I missed the coverage.

I also don't watch the local news. Unlike the local newspapers, our two local television stations—WGAL 8 and WPMT Fox 43—are both run by monkeys. At least, that's the way it seems to me. Channel 8 spends fifty-five minutes of every news hour extolling the benefits of their Super Doppler Weather Radar. The remaining five minutes are usually devoted to a special feature regarding whichever advertiser paid them the most money that week. I'm not kidding about this. Fox 43 isn't much better. To their credit, they do attempt to report the news, but their idea of reporting involves sending pretty female news anchors out to the local dairy farm or Cub Scout meeting for some 'slice of life' events. If Iran does eventually build a nuclear bomb, you won't hear about it on either station, because Channel 8 will have local weatherman Doug Allen jerking off over the goddamn Super Doppler Radar and Fox 43 will be reporting live from some craft fair in fucking Hanover.

I don't know if either of them reported on the accident. I somehow doubt it, but if they did, I missed the report.

And don't even get me started on the sorry state of our local radio stations…

In truth, even though it was only twenty-four hours since I'd swept up the debris, I'd already forgotten all about the crash. After all, it had happened while I was gone, and none of the victims were anyone that I knew, and our property hadn't been damaged, and the wreckage was gone, so it didn't really impact me that much. It was something that happened, a momentary distraction, but there were other things to focus on, important things like writing and trying to figure out if it was possible to add yet another novel to my list of deadlines in order to pay for the baby's daycare.

Perhaps that sounds callous. Someone had lost their life. Perhaps I should have been a little more concerned. Caring. Sympathetic. But I wasn't. I don't think that makes me a bad person. I think it just makes me what I am—a flawed human, just like everybody else.

Around noon, I walked up to the top of the driveway to get the mail. I noticed a rustic, white picket cross and a beautiful floral arrangement mounted on the smashed guardrail. I've driven by these crosses countless times. You see them dotting our roads and interstates. Sometimes, they seem almost as abundant as McDonald's, Exxon and other highway staples. I'd never actually seen one up close, though. Up until that moment, I'd only experienced them as a passing glance through the windshield, there but for the blink of an eye and then gone as the next mile marker rolled past.

Curious, I quickly pulled the mail out of our mailbox and then hurried over to the cross for a closer look. The flowers were fresh and professionally arranged. There was no tag or any indication of which local florist had put them together. Nor was there a name on the cross. Not even the old standard 'R.I.P.' It was just plain white—two thin slats nailed together in the middle.

I turned away and started back downhill. The mailman had brought no royalty or advance checks. Instead, there were only bills, catalogs and my monthly issues of *National Geographic*, *Soldier of Fortune* and *The Fortean Times* (all of which, for some inexplicable reason, seem to arrive on the same day each month). I was flipping through the bills, wondering how the hell we were going to stay caught up on them, when the wind began to blow. I heard a rustling sound behind me.

Figuring it was my cat, Max (who lives outdoors and was the source of inspiration for Hannibal from my short story, "Halves"), I turned around and then stopped.

Ever see the wind pick up a bunch of leaves and spin them in a mini-cyclone? It's common, of course. That's what was happening. The leaves around the cross were spinning fast, reaching a height of about five and a half feet off the ground. Then, as quickly as it had started, the breeze died off and the leaves floated back down to the ground.

That was the first thing that happened. I didn't think much about it at the time, and even now, I'm almost willing to chalk it up to nothing more than a natural occurrence—except for everything that's happened since then.

In hindsight, there was nothing about it that was natural…

ENTRY 7:

The second thing that happened is also somewhat dubious, but when considered in the greater context, it makes me wonder, especially given her recent expressed desire to move.

Cassi is a smoker. Ever since the baby came along, she only smokes outside, and then, only after he's gone to bed. There's an ashtray out on the deck, along with a table, four chairs and the glider. Oh yes, we can't forget about the porch glider. It's the central part of our story.

The glider is a family heirloom. It belonged to Cassi's grandmother and was given to us after she passed away. Cassi has fond memories of sitting on it when she was a little girl. It's very comfortable, but the cushions are a garish, green floral print and when it rains, they soak up the moisture. Sit on them after a storm and your ass will get wet.

Within two days of the accident, Cassi stopped smoking out on the deck. Instead, she began smoking in our bathroom with the door closed and the exhaust fan running full blast. At first, I didn't think anything of it. Keep in mind, it was winter. I just assumed that it was too cold outside to smoke. But as months passed and the nights grew warmer, she still avoided smoking out on the deck. When I asked her why, she said she got spooked out there at night. Neither our flashlight nor the big dusk-to-dawn light that's installed on the side of the garage helped. She said it was still too dark out there, and sometimes, she felt like someone was watching her. Despite those lights, the top of our driveway remains pitch black at night. If you shine the flashlight up the hill, the beam gets lost in the darkness, almost as if the shadows are swallowing it. The only thing that dispels the darkness are the headlights of approaching cars, and then, only for an instant.

I asked her when she'd started feeling this way, and she said it was after the accident.

My wife is not given to flights of fancy. She's firmly

grounded in reality. She's the Agent Scully to my Agent Mulder, to put it in terms of *The X-Files*. The only spiritual or supernatural activity she even remotely engages in is occasionally attending Catholic or Episcopalian church services. She doesn't believe in aliens or Bigfoot or the Loch Ness Monster or ghosts. Despite this, being out on our deck and staring up at the driveway at night has made her uncomfortable enough to start smoking inside. As I write this, many months later, that is still her practice. Let's call that occurrence number two, and catalog it accordingly.

ENTRY 8:

If this were a horror novel, I'd plot it like one, but it's not a horror novel. It's simply a diary, notating a random collection of occurrences, all of which have happened since the accident. I'm jumping around here. One minute, I'm in the present. The next, I'm back to the beginning again. There is no linear narrative. There is no slow build of suspense and dread. There is only me, trying to make sense of it all.

I can't remember who said it, but there's a great quote regarding *The Amityville Horror*, *Poltergeist* and similar haunted house stories. The quote (and I'm paraphrasing here) goes something like this: 'If this stuff really happened, if the house was really haunted, then why did the people stay? Why didn't they move the fuck out as soon as they heard the voices/saw the ghost/the dog started levitating? Because that's what would happen in real life.'

Except that's not true. I know, because this is real life. This is real fucking life and we can't move. We can't move because we can't afford to move. We can't afford to buy another house. Cassi's been talking about it again—talking about finding a place with sidewalks and fenced-in backyards where the baby can play. A year ago, she was fine with him growing up playing in our big backyard with its trees and trout stream and wild outdoors. Now she's craving suburbia, and I think I know why. I don't think it has anything to do with sidewalks. It has to do with some of the things that have happened here.

That should make me happy, because if it's true, then it means that I'm not crazy. If she's experiencing things too—enough that she suddenly wants to move—then that's proof right there that I'm not losing my mind. Right? If so, then I should be ecstatic. But I'm not. I'm not because this is my family we're talking about, and we probably should move and I can't afford to do it. I'm supposed to take care of them and provide for them and protect them, and in this case, the best way to do those things is to buy another house and get the hell away from here.

I wish sometimes that I still had a real job, a job where I operated a machine or moved boxes around, and got a paycheck every week for my efforts. A job with health insurance and a 401K would be nice, too. It would be awesome to have a job where people didn't email me at the end of the day, after I busted my ass for eight hours, and say, "Your last book sucked. When are you gonna write another zombie novel?" But I'd even put up with that, as long as the job gave me a steady enough income that I could buy us a new home.

Earlier this week, I tried to get a job like that. I went back to two of my former employers—the foundry and the loading docks. Neither one of them were hiring, on account of the economy. The Human Resources Director at the foundry said, "You must be a millionaire from all those books. Why would you want to come back to work here?"

Life is nothing more than a series of lyrics from Bruce Springsteen songs.

This is good whiskey. Woodford Reserve. Big fucking bottle. I believe I will have some more. I believe, in fact, that I will drink this bottle dry tonight.

The people in those stories don't move out because they can't. They're trapped.

So am I.

ENTRY 9:

The third bit of strangeness occurred around the end of March. In truth, I'd again forgotten all about the accident. Oh, sure, I thought of it for a second when I went up to get the mail or pulled in or out of my driveway. The cross was kind of hard to miss. The floral arrangements had since withered and died, but the marker was still there. So while I did occasionally think of the accident, such thoughts were fleeting. They weren't even fully-formed thoughts. If anything, they were just echoes.

I'd even forgotten about the mini-cyclone the leaves had formed. Cassi had taken to smoking inside, but as I said earlier, I hadn't put two and two together at that point, and didn't know why she'd changed her routine. I thought it was because of the cold weather.

The third occurrence was an incredibly vivid and detailed dream. I know that I dream all night. I've been told by Cassi, ex-girlfriends, my ex-wife, one-night stands, cellmates, my old Navy buddies and anyone else who has ever slept beside me that I'm restless at night. I kick and twitch and talk in my sleep. Not mumbling. Not whispering. No, I have loud, boisterous and elaborate dream conversations. Sadly, I never remember them. It's rare that I remember any of my dreams. But I remembered this one. It happened in March. Here we are, months later, and I still remember every detail.

In the dream, I was sitting out on our deck after dark, smoking a cigar and looking up at the stars twinkling down through the tree limbs. I do this quite a bit in the waking world, so the dream was pleasant enough. Max was sprawled in my lap, and I was petting him with one hand and holding my cigar in the other. My dog, Sam (who was the inspiration for Big Steve in my novel *Dark Hollow*, as well as many other things), was sprawled at my feet. There was a glass of bourbon on the table in front of me. Crickets and spring peepers were chirping over in the swamp, and in the distance, I could hear the soft, muted roar of the trout stream. Eventually, I became aware that Max and I weren't alone. I heard the glider rails squeak, as if someone was slowly rocking back and forth. I turned around and there was a girl sitting on the glider. As soon as I saw her, Max jumped down off my lap and ran away, hissing.

The girl was young, maybe eighteen or nineteen years old. She had long, shoulder-length blonde hair, combed straight. She was thin but not skinny. Pretty. She wore denim jeans, sneakers and a white t-shirt. She clutched a black cell phone in one hand, and held it at her side, as if waiting for it to ring. When she raised her head and looked at me, her expression was one of profound sadness.

She said something, but I couldn't hear her. Her lips moved silently.

And then I woke up. I lay there for a while, thinking about the dream and wondering what it meant. Did I know the girl? She seemed vaguely familiar, but I didn't know why. I was left with a sense—a certainty—that I *should* know her, and yet I didn't. Who was she? Could she have been a fan I'd met at a book signing, perhaps? Or maybe someone I'd encountered briefly at some point in my life, but had since forgotten—an old coworker or one-night stand?

I didn't know, and the harder I thought about it, the more important it seemed.

Unable to sleep, I slipped out of bed, pissed, and then put on my robe. I went out to my office, made a pot of coffee and worked until five o'clock in the morning, at which point I came in and waited for the baby to wake up. When he did, I got him out of the crib, changed his diaper and made him breakfast. When Cassi finally woke up, she was grateful for the opportunity to sleep in. She asked me what time I'd gotten up, and I told her. Then I told her about the dream. She agreed that it was odd.

A new day began, but unlike the leaf cyclone or the accident itself, I didn't forget about the dream. I jotted it down in my commonplace book (a notebook that many authors use to write down story ideas, scraps of dialogue, plot devices, sketches, or anything else that occurs to them when they are away from their writing instruments) with the intent of cannibalizing it for a story at some point in the future. There was something about the dream. Something unsettling. I wanted to capture every detail. I needed to make sure that I would remember her face.

What I didn't know at the time was that remembering her face wouldn't be a problem for me, because I would see her again.

ENTRY 10:

About two weeks after that, I was sitting out on the deck with Sam and Max. It was early April, and quite a warm evening for the season. Much like in the dream, I was smoking a cigar, drinking bourbon and watching the stars. I even remember what brands the cigar and bourbon were—Partagas 1845 Black Label and Knob Creek with just a little bit of ice. Max was sprawled in my lap, all twenty pounds of him, purring and stretching and acting not at all like the badass outdoor tomcat he likes to portray himself as when others are around. Sam was lying at my feet, leash-free, but to keep him on the porch, I'd strategically placed two baby gates at each of the deck's exits. Had I not done this, Sam would have waited until I was distracted and then dashed off into the woods. He is a mutt—mostly a mix of Rottweiler and Beagle, the latter of which comes out in him whenever he catches a scent. We walk quite often through the woods and whenever he sniffs a rabbit or a fox or any other creature, he strains at the leash hard enough to choke himself. On the few occasions where he's actually slipped his collar, he runs off without thought of consequence, totally focused and consumed on tracking his quarry. Usually, he ends up lost and exhausted to the point of collapse, and I have to hunt him down and carry him back home. The baby gates prevented that, and allowed me to enjoy my cigar and whiskey in peace. Cassi was inside, talking on the phone to J. F. "Jesus" Gonzalez's wife. The baby was asleep. All was right with the world.

I was sitting there smoking and thinking about literary estates. Jesus and I had both been wanting to create literary estates for our families. I was pretty sure that was what Cassi and her friend were discussing, as well, because in addition to the literary estates, we wanted to legally draft an agreement wherein if either Cassi and I or Jesus and his wife died unexpectedly, we would gain legal guardianship over the other's children. Cassi was of a mind that we didn't need to worry about things like that yet, but I wasn't so sure. Both of our parents are too old to care full-time for a child, and my oldest son, who was eighteen at the time, had his whole life ahead of him. It didn't seem right to burden him with the possibility of having to care for his younger half-brother, should something happen to us.

Creating a literary estate took money, something that neither Jesus nor I had much of. I'd gotten a sample draft from a link Neil Gaiman had posted, and was weighing the possibilities of finding something similar on LegalZoom.com or another website. I wondered if such a document would still be considered legal. This was important to me. I didn't want to die and have the rights to my work fall into the hands of one of my publishers. The money, what little there was, should go to my sons.

This was what I was thinking about when Sam started growling. I glanced down at him. He was staring at the top of the driveway. His ears were flattened and his haunches were raised. His tail was between his legs and he stood stiff as a board. When I reached for him, he growled again. His eyes never left the spot at the top of the hill.

I looked around, thinking he'd seen an animal, but the driveway was deserted. Annoyed, I picked up Max, sat him down and then took Sam inside. When I came back out, Max had run off to the garage and was standing outside the door, meowing to be let in. Although he is an outdoor cat, Max sleeps in the garage at night. It provides him safety from the cold in the winter and protection from nocturnal predators like coyotes and foxes and owls in the warmer months. I opened the door and let him in. Then I closed it behind me and returned to my cigar.

As I sat down again, the porch glider began to move. The rocking was slow, but noticeable. Back and forth. Back and forth. The aluminum struts squeaked. Max began howling inside the garage. In the house, I heard Sam start growling again. He barked once, loud and powerful. Then Cassi hollered at him to shut up. Her voice was muted, almost lost beneath the forcefulness of his bark. Through it all, the glider kept rocking. There was no wind. I glanced up at the treetops to confirm this. No wind, not even a slight breeze. Sometimes, when a dump truck or tractor trailer goes barreling down the road, they'll vibrate our deck, but the road was clear. There were no vibrations, no disturbance.

And yet the glider was moving.

I said, "What the fuck?"

The glider's rails squeaked in response as it continued rocking. Cigar clenched between my teeth, I walked over to it. It stopped moving when I was halfway across the deck.

If this was fiction, this would be the part of the story where the protagonist starts to put two and two together—

the dream of the girl on the glider (so eerily similar in setting to what was now occurring in real life), the glider moving on its own while the protagonist watches. But this isn't fiction, and I didn't put those two events together. Not then.

That came after my son started saying "Hi" to something I couldn't see.

ENTRY 11:

Been a few days since I worked on this. Real life intruded. To paraphrase Bob Segar, deadlines and commitments, what to leave in and what to leave out. I finished the extra material for *Darkness on the Edge of Town* tonight. It's a little after 3am and I'm sitting here wondering how "Bounce, Rock, Skate, Roll" by Vaughan Mason & Crew ended up in my iTunes library. I've got about ten-thousand songs on iTunes, the culmination of a lifelong music collection, and when I write, I put them on random shuffle. It makes for eclectic and inspiring background music. I never know what will pop up next. Jerry Reed and then Anthrax, followed by The Alan Parsons Project and then Marvin Gaye and then Public Enemy and then Johnny Cash or Guns N' Roses or Neil Diamond or Iron Maiden or Alice In Chains or Dr. Dre. But I don't remember ever owning this disco tune, and here it is, blasting from my computer's speakers and subwoofer.

I don't have a lot in life. Material wealth has not accompanied my success, and these days, I seem to have more hangers-on and acquaintances than I do real friends, but the one thing I've got going for me is a kick-ass collection of tunes. And an awesome fucking library. This is what I leave behind for my sons—a metric fuck-ton of books, comics and music.

Anyway, I went back through this tonight, reading what I wrote, and I noticed something. Even in this, my secret diary, I avoid mentioning the baby's name. When he was born, Cassi and I made a decision to guard his privacy as much as possible. We've never posted a picture of him online. Indeed, when I do talk about him in public, I refer to him as 'Turtle,' rather than his real name. Maybe we're just being paranoid, but I don't care. I've got enough crazies out there, and have gotten enough death threats that I'm not taking any chances. Like I said at the beginning, I genuinely half-expect to get done in by some crazed 'fan' one of these days. What's to stop Nicky, the guy who said he wanted to, (quote) "shoot me in the head with a crossbow because I psychically stole his story ideas" (end quote) from hopping on a Greyhound and coming to York County and tracking down my kid at school? These are the thoughts that keep a horror writer awake at night. So we guard his identity, and I did it even here, in this Word document, and I wasn't even aware I was doing it until now.

I would do anything for my sons. I would murder others to keep them safe. My oldest son, David, is now an adult and can fend for himself. He's as big of a genre geek as I am, and he likes telling goth girls who his dad is, in hopes of getting laid. And it works, too. He gets more game at sci-fi and horror conventions than Coop and I ever did back in the day. I don't have to worry about him as much anymore. He's a smart kid…hell, he's not even a kid. He's a man, now. But I still have to worry about my youngest son. The world is a scary place and he has no fear. When he attempts to climb out of his crib, he isn't aware that he might fall. When he clambers up onto the couch and rolls around, he doesn't realize that he could tumble off. He is not afraid of the electrical outlets or the neighbor's dog or the swift, deep and powerful stream running through our property. He has no fear of strangers. He greets everyone he meets by waving his little hand in the air, smiling broadly until his dimples overshadow the rest of his face, and then shouting "Hi."

Which is what he did the morning after I saw the glider moving by itself.

My mother was watching him for the day, and I had just brought him out of the house to take him over to her place. I was walking across the deck, juggling the baby and the diaper bag and a travel mug full of coffee and my car keys, when the baby suddenly whipped his head around, waved at the glider and shouted an enthusiastic greeting.

"Hi!"

Little hand waving back and forth just as fast as it could go. Big smile showing off those baby teeth. Eyes sparkling. My kid is a charmer, but there was nobody there to charm— at least that I could see.

"Hi," he said again, as if he was speaking to someone he knew. When I turned toward the glider, I saw that it was moving. It stopped as I gave it my full attention, as if it had been rocking back and forth unnoticed, and the person doing it had gotten up when I focused my attention on it. That was when I started to get creeped the fuck out.

I carried the baby down to the car, and as I opened the back door and bent over to strap him into his car seat, he looked over my shoulder, waved again and shouted "Hi" a third time. He was staring at the top of the driveway.

Inside the house, Sam howled.

My hands and fingers felt numb. I fumbled with the straps on the car seat. Once the baby was safely inside, I started the car. Howard Stern came on, but I didn't pay any attention to him. I was too busy putting it all together in my head. The car wreck. The leaf cyclone at the top of the driveway. Cassi getting spooked out on our deck. The weird dream I'd had. The porch glider moving on its own. And now this.

I drove slowly to the top of the driveway. I stopped, looking both ways for oncoming traffic before pulling out. The makeshift monument was still there. The flowers were dead and gone, but the cross remained—a lone reminder of what had occurred there. I bit my lip, waiting for the baby to wave at the cross and say hi, but he didn't. He was busy playing with a pacifier. In hindsight, I'm glad he didn't.

If he had, I think I might have screamed.

* * *

I dropped him off at my mom's, and then stopped in to see Bill Wahl and Ned Senft (some old friends of mine who are the proprietors of Comix Connection, a Central-Pennsylvanian chain of comic book stores). It turned out that Bill and Ned weren't in that day. Manager Jared Wolf was working the counter. He was his usual friendly, gregarious self, but I found it hard to talk. My mind wasn't on comic books. It was on what had just happened. It must have been obvious because before I left the store, Jared asked me if I was feeling okay.

When I got home, I considered ripping that stupid cross

out of the ground and tossing it over the bridge and into the creek. I imagined it floating along on the current until it ended up in the Susquehanna River, and then bobbed along until ultimately landing in the chemical stew that is the Chesapeake Bay, and from there into the Atlantic Ocean. Or maybe taking it down and smashing it in the road. Or driving over it. Or setting it on fire. Or using it for target practice.

But I did none of these things. I put it out of my mind. There was weirdness afoot, and it seemed to me that the best thing to do was to ignore it. I told myself these were nothing more than a string of coincidences, and the only reason I suspected something more sinister was because of what I did for a living.

I got out of the car and went to work. At the end of the day, I drove back to my mother's house and picked up the baby. When we got home, and I got him out of the car, he glanced at the top of the driveway, now half-hidden in the encroaching evening gloom, and said, "Hi." When he waved, I peered into the shadows, wondering if something was waving back at him.

* * *

He's done that ever since—every single day. Every time we bring him outside, he waves at the top of the driveway and says, "Hi." One night, when he woke at 3am and absolutely refused to go back to sleep, I took him out to the car. Sometimes, driving him around will make him sleep when nothing else will. It was pitch black outside. There was no moon. No stars. No light of any kind. We literally couldn't see five feet in front of us, let alone the top of the driveway. That was the only time he didn't do it.

Cassi says he's talking to the passing trucks, or our neighbor's goat, or a variety of other things, none of which are supernatural. I've never told her who I suspect the baby is saying hi to.

ENTRY 12:

Things went on like that for a while. There were no more leaf cyclones and the glider didn't move, but the baby still waved and said hello every morning, and I still had weird dreams some nights. They were always the same—the girl sitting on the glider, staring at her cell phone with a sad expression.

I didn't do anything about it. I mean, stop and think about it for a minute. What could I do? Call an exorcist? That shit only works in the movies. In real life, I wouldn't know where to start. I couldn't very well call up the Vatican and say, "Hi, this is mid-list horror novelist Brian Keene. I'd like to hire an exorcist to come chase a ghost away from my house." And although I know some occultists and ghost hunters, I couldn't ask them for advice either. Mason Winfield and Bob Freeman would have probably been happy to come check it out, but Mason is near Buffalo and Bob lives out in Indiana, and I couldn't afford their travel and lodging expenses. It would have been embarrassing to ask them for help and then tell them it would have to be on their own dime. Vince Harper, former head of Bereshith Publishing and Shadowlands Press, was closer, and as far as I knew he was still involved in the OTO, but I had no idea how to get in touch with him. He'd sort of fallen off the grid after leaving his publishing gig in the horror genre. I still miss him. Vince was a good guy, and these days, good guys are in short supply in this business.

The main reason I didn't act, however, was because I just didn't believe it. It's one thing to write fictional stories about ghosts. It's something very different to actually believe those things are occurring to you in real life. That's the appeal of horror fiction. In real life, the monsters are the ones abducting and killing children or flying hijacked airplanes into skyscrapers or looting our treasury and sending our kids off to fight a bullshit war just so they can line their own pockets and the pockets of their corporate buddies or eradicating our Bill of Rights in the name of national security. Those are the real monsters. Watch an hour of that shit on CNN or MSNBC or FOX and you're more than ready to curl up with a fictional monster. Zombies, werewolves, vampires and ghosts are an escape from the real world because they don't exist in the real world.

Except that I was apparently being confronted with proof of a ghost's existence, and since that was impossible, the only other option was to question my sanity—which was no option at all. No way could I be going crazy. I had too many fucking books to finish. Insanity is not conducive to meeting deadlines, nor does it provide for one's family.

So I forced myself to ignore all of it. The dreams were just that—dreams. And Cassi was right. The baby was just saying hi to the neighbor's goat and the trucks racing by. These are the things I told myself, and they worked, for the most part...

...until I heard the cell phone.

It was a Wednesday night. The baby was asleep. Cassi

and I were curled up on the couch, watching the final season of *The Shield*. I'd seen all of the episodes already, but she could never stay awake late enough to watch them on their original air-dates, so I'd bought the whole season on DVD when it came out. I love *The Shield*. I genuinely believe that it, along with *The Sopranos* and *The Wire*, is the best series ever on television. Vic Mackey is a perfect example of how to write a sympathetic character. He's an absolutely loathsome individual, and yet we, the viewers, root for him every week. That is great writing.

But I digress. Anyway, we were watching *The Shield*. Vic was busy stabbing Ronnie in the back when I got up and went into the kitchen to get a bottle of water. Since I'd seen the episode already, I didn't pause the DVD. I opened the refrigerator, reached inside for a bottle, and that was when I heard the beeping. At first, I ignored it. A lifetime of heavy metal concerts, military service, and shooting guns on the weekend with Coop and Jesus, as well as hereditary hearing loss, has left me with all kinds of weird little sounds in my ears. Usually, it's a ringing noise. It comes and goes. It seems at its worst when I'm tired or drunk.

The sound I heard now was different. I stood there, cool mist swirling out of the open refrigerator, and listened. The baby has a toy cell phone that beeps and rings when you push the buttons. I thought that perhaps Smokey (my wife's indoor cat) was playing with it. She's not yet a year old and still has a lot of kitten in her, and she likes to play with the baby's toys. Turn your back for one second and she's wandering off with his Curious George doll or batting a block around on the floor. After a few seconds, it occurred to me that I couldn't be hearing the baby's toy phone because we'd picked up all his toys before he went to bed—a nightly ritual we make sure to engage him in. I sing the "Clean Up" song from *Barney* while we do it. I use a Barney voice because it makes the baby laugh.

That wasn't what was happening this time, but there was no way to tell her that. I walked up to the window and looked out into the darkness. Our porch light, which is motion sensitive and comes on even when something as small as a squirrel runs by, was dark. The beeping continued, and it wasn't my imagination. The sound was coming from the glider.

"Do you want me to pause this?"

I jumped, startled. Cassi was standing between the kitchen and the living room. When I turned around, I saw that her expression was puzzled.

"What are you doing?"

I shrugged. "I thought I heard something."

"What?"

"It sounded like…a cell phone. You know, like when someone is dialing or texting? The little beeps that the keys make?"

She paused, frowning. "I don't hear it."

That's what I'm afraid of, I thought to myself.

"You want to go outside and check it out?" she asked.

"No," I said. "It was probably nothing."

* * *

One week later, I was hauling the trash cans up to the road so that the garbage men could pick them up the next morning. It was dark out, and I had a flashlight in one hand so that speeding cars wouldn't plow into me.

At the top of the driveway, I heard the beeping sound again.

I've written about characters feeling "an icy finger running up their spine" but until that moment, I'd never experienced it in real life. Indeed, I didn't think it was something you actually *could* experience in real life. I'd always thought it was just one of those standard euphemisms that are occasionally required in horror fiction.

I shined the flashlight around, but there was nobody there. It was just me, the trees, our mailbox, our neighbor's mailbox and trash cans, and that wooden cross, now looking much more weather-beaten and worse for the wear.

The beeping stopped.

I leaned the trash cans against the guardrail and the beeping recommenced. Headlights pinpointed me, and I heard a pickup truck come around the corner. It zipped past me fast enough to ruffle my jacket. After it had passed, and the darkness returned, the road was silent.

"There's nothing there," I said out loud.

I started down the driveway and the beeping rang out behind me.

I ran all the way to the deck. I was out of breath when I got inside. Cassi asked me what was wrong. I smiled and waved a hand, indicating that I'd answer her as soon as I'd stopped hyperventilating. When I could talk again, I lied, and told her that I ran down the driveway to get some exercise.

ENTRY 13:

The dreams continued sporadically throughout the spring and into the summer. With them came more glider rocking and phantom texting during my waking hours. If they had happened every day, I really do think I would have lost my shit, but they didn't. There was no rhyme or reason. No way of predicting when it would occur. Weeks would go by without a single nightmare and then I'd have four in a row. A month would pass without the glider moving on its own or those haunting, disembodied beeps, and then there would be a flurry of activity that lasted several days.

There were little things, too—occasional, one-time occurrences that didn't seem connected to all of this at the time, but certainly do now, in hindsight.

Example 1: The baby has this toy locomotive. It's big. He can push it along and walk behind it, or sit atop it and scoot along with his feet. It has all kinds of buttons and little animal figures that pop out of the side. Every time it moves or you press a button, the train sings (loudly) "Chugga chugga, choo choo, spin around. Every letter has a sound." Annoying, yes. Thank God it only plays the song once. If the baby wants to hear it again, he has to push it or press another button.

One afternoon, while the baby was at his grandparent's house, Cassi and I went grocery shopping. When we came home, the locomotive was playing the song, over and over and over again. There was nobody home at the time. The dog was cowering on the couch, staring at it, and the cat was hiding in the bedroom. We had to take the batteries out to get it to stop. I didn't chalk it up to the girl on the glider. I attributed it to "the dog or the cat must have bumped it and the song got stuck and just kept repeating." When we put new batteries in it, the locomotive operated normally again.

"Chugga chugga, choo choo, spin around. Every letter has a sound."

I can't stand that fucking train.

Example 2: In late May, I was working out in my office one night. I can't remember if I mentioned this before or not (and I'm too lazy to go back and check) but my office is separate from the house. If someone were to walk down my driveway, they would pass by my office before they reached the house. Anyway, I'm sitting there writing something (I can't remember what) and Max, who was curled up on my lap, suddenly jumps down, runs over to the wall, arches his back and hisses. Had someone been on the other side of that wall, they would have been standing in my driveway. Max hissed again and when I went to him, I found that he was inconsolable. I grabbed my Taurus .357 and hurried outside, expecting to find a coyote or another stray cat or maybe some crazed fan standing in my driveway.

But there was nothing.

There are a lot more of these examples, but it's late and I'm tired and I don't have time tonight to put them all down on paper. Suffice to say, it was a weird few months.

Was I scared? Well, of course I was fucking scared. You would be, too. Either our house was haunted or I was losing my goddamn mind, and since I wasn't the type to believe in ghosts, and since Cassi or my friends or my neighbor hadn't reported hearing anything weird or seeing anything unusual, option number two was looking more and more likely every day.

In early June, I decided that I'd been hallucinating all this time. I became convinced that I had a brain tumor, and that was what was causing the hallucinations. It seemed plausible enough. Tumors had popped up elsewhere on my body that summer. If spring is the growing season, then my body had a bumper crop. There were a total of nineteen, all of which had quite literally sprung up in just a couple of weeks. They were scattered throughout my body—arms, chest, abdomen, thighs, and elsewhere. The smallest was about the size of a marble. The biggest was like a ping pong ball.

Needless to say, I was scared—scared in ways that a self-rocking glider and phantom cell phone tones couldn't begin to touch. Obviously, I had cancer. I mean, what else could the tumors be? I wondered how I'd gotten them. My dad's exposure to Agent Orange in Vietnam, perhaps? Or maybe it was the fact that I've used tobacco since I was twelve and I drink like a fucking fish? Eventually, I decided it didn't really matter how I'd gotten cancer. The how wasn't important. What mattered was what happened next.

It was a strange summer. I felt like I'd become one of my own characters. I was Tommy O'Brien from *Terminal* or Harold Newton from "Marriage Causes Cancer In Rats." I was meant to be working on novels and novellas and short stories and comic books for a variety of small press and mainstream publishers who would dick around with my paycheck, my rights, and everything else. Instead, I found myself facing mortality and, for the first time, considering—I mean really considering—my own eventual death. I made sure all my shit was in order. Talked with Nate Southard and Mike Oliveri and brought them up to speed on where everything was (because if I did die, they'd be best suited to finish any uncompleted manuscripts). Checked into my life insurance policy and made sure it was up-to-date.

And then I went to the doctor. He was less than comforting. He said it could be cancer, or it could be something called lipoma—a benign tumor composed of fatty tissue. I asked him if he could be any more specific, if perhaps he could narrow it down to one or the other. He said that he couldn't, but that a specialist could. So I went to see the specialist. He said it was most certainly lipoma and that normally, that wouldn't be a concern, but in my case, several of the tumors were growing toward major organs, including my heart, liver and kidneys. So he sent me to see a surgeon. It turned out that the surgeon, the anesthesiologist, and one of the girls who ran the office were all fans of my work. On the day of my surgery, the three of them brought books for me to sign. I did. Then they knocked me out and I went under the knife. They removed ten of the nineteen growths, including a particularly nasty fucker that had, according to the surgeon, grown its own circulatory system and was sending tendrils toward my heart.

And then we were done.

It's human nature to go back to doing what one was doing before, but I didn't. Instead, I became preoccupied with death. What happens after this, you know? Is there really an afterlife? Does our consciousness—our spirit or soul—continue after it leaves our body, or do we just become worm food? Is there a God, Allah, Krishna, Cthulhu, etc.? Is there a Heaven or a Hell, and if so, where would I go? I don't know which scares me more—that there is an afterlife and I might end up in the bad part of town, or that there's nothing after this and that all of life's struggles are ultimately pointless. What if everything we know, every person we've loved, every kiss we've shared, every tear we've shed, fight we've had, breath we've taken, every laugh and shout and orgasm and idea and everything else that constitutes life just doesn't fucking matter the moment our heart stops beating and our brainwaves go flat? Which is it? Where is the proof? I've thought about this all year, and I'm no closer to an answer. All I know is that I don't want to die. I think I might have developed a death phobia. I'm terrified of dying.

There's one more occurrence to write about. One more example of the weirdness that has infected my home and my life. The incident with the baby monitor. That's the biggie, and once I've written about it, we'll be all up to date.

But I still have no idea what it all means. It turned out I didn't have a brain tumor after all, so if these things are hallucinations, then they're being caused by something else. In truth, I suspect they aren't hallucinations, which takes us back to the beginning—and means that I'm either being haunted, or I'm crazy.

Before we tackle that, though, I should write about the baby monitor.

Tomorrow. Sleep now. Tired. Mid-life crisis, maybe? Feel old. Feel older every goddamn day. Creeping toward an ultimate end.

A sense of finality seems to hang over everything I do.

ENTRY 14:

Haven't worked on this in quite some time. Caught in the perfect storm of deadlines and a cash crunch, I fucked off to the wilderness and got some things done before I snapped and started shooting motherfuckers. Cassi was the one who suggested that I do this. It was a week before Thanksgiving and I was under a lot of stress. *A Gathering of Crows* was three months overdue, and although my editor, Don D'Auria, was being incredibly gracious and understanding in regards to the missed deadline, I felt like I was letting him down. Don is one of the few editors who has always been straight with me, and it bothers me to think I might disappoint him in any way (and I'm sure it bothers him that his superiors owe me a bunch of money for previous novels—novels for which the deadline wasn't missed).

But it wasn't just one missed deadline. I'd have been able to cope with that. In addition to *A Gathering of Crows*, I owed Maurice Broaddus a story for an anthology called *Dark Faith*, a novel synopsis to Bantam, two issues of *The Last Zombie* to the guys at Antarctic Press, a television treatment that I knew wasn't going to go anywhere, two comic book pitches that I also suspected would go nowhere, and assorted other things. Gak was waiting on me to finish *The Wanderer*. I owed Full Moon Press a novella of some sort that I couldn't even remember signing a contract for. Wrath, Bev Vincent, Steven Shrewsbury, Tim Lebbon, Bryan Smith and Jim Moore were all waiting on me to finish my collaboration with Nick Mamatas so that I could work on the collaborations I'd promised that I'd eventually do with them. Plus, there were signature sheets to be signed, introductions to write even though I keep telling people I don't have time to write introductions, three months' worth of email to answer, a message board to keep up with, weekly installments of *Earthworm Gods II: Deluge* (lest people bitch about it not being updated), and somewhere in-between all of this, trying to be a father to my sons, a friend to my friends, and a husband to my wife. It had also been six months since anybody had paid me. Oh, they all wanted their manuscripts on time, but when it came time to send me my fucking check, that was a different fucking story.

I'd also become distinctly aware that a number of people who I'd thought were my friends were my friends only because of *who* I am and not because of who I *am*. There is a distinction there, and I bet Stephen King, Dean Koontz, or Richard Laymon would have commiserated. But I wasn't going to ask King and Koontz for advice on shit like that, simply because I know how overwhelming it is when people do it to me. And Dick Laymon wasn't around to ask anymore. I considered trying to contact him via an Ouija board or a medium. Ask him for advice on how to deal with all of the users and abusers and hangers-on in my life, and "Hey, Dick, while we're at it, what can you tell me about the afterlife? Because I've got to tell you, my old mentor—I'm fucking scared of dying."

Oh, did I mention there were more tumors that needed to be removed?

I was stressed. That's an understatement. In truth, I'd reached the breaking point. Cassi caught me applying for a part-time job at Walmart, and she sat me down and said, "You are going to the family cabin in West Virginia and you're not coming back until you clear your head."

"I can't," I told her. "It's almost Thanksgiving."

"I don't care. All we're doing for Thanksgiving is going to my parents' house, and they make you uncomfortable anyway. I'd much rather you went off to the cabin and got some writing done and felt better about life."

So I did. I took the dog down to our cabin in West

Virginia and I stayed there for ten days and all I did was write and eat and sleep.

When I returned home, I was a different man. No, scratch that. The Brian Keene who had gone to the cabin was a different man. When I came home, I was me again. Reborn. Refreshed. Rejuvenated.

But there was still one thing left unfinished.

The baby monitor story.

* * *

Here is an example of how I cannibalize real life for use in my fiction. I've said in interviews that everything is fodder for my muse, and I'm not kidding when I say that.

The following scene is from *A Gathering of Crows*. I wrote it after the real-life incident with the baby monitor:

Artie Prater slept, which was exactly what he'd been afraid of. His wife of five years, Laura, was out of town. She worked for the bank in Roncefort, and once a year, all of the bank's employees went on a mandatory week-long retreat. This year, they were in Utah, enjoying steak dinners and attending seminars about things like team-building and synergy. Artie liked to tease Laura about these things, but only because he was secretly jealous. He'd been unable to find work for over a year, and it bothered him that he couldn't provide for his wife or their new son, Artie Junior. The upside was that while she was at work every day, he'd been able to stay home and take care of Little Artie. Laura reciprocated by getting up with the baby at night, which relieved Artie to no end.

Artie had always been a deep sleeper. His mother had once said that he could sleep through a nuclear war, and that wasn't far from the truth. He'd slept through 9/11, waking up in his college dorm room later that night and wondering why everyone was staring at the television and crying. Since becoming a father, Artie's biggest fear was that the baby would wake up crying, perhaps hungry or in need of a diaper change or shaking from a nightmare, and he'd sleep through it. That's why he was grateful when Laura was there to get up with Artie Junior at night, and that's why he dreaded these rare times when she wasn't home.

They had a baby monitor in the house. A small camera was mounted above Little Artie's crib. It broadcast a signal to the monitor, which was plugged into the bedroom's television. With Laura out of town, Artie had turned the volume on the television all the way up, filling the room with white noise and the soft sounds of his son's breathing. Then, bathed in the glow from the screen, he'd sat back in bed with his laptop and played a video game. It was early—too early to sleep, but Little Artie had been tired and cranky, and Artie knew from experience that he should rest when the baby rested. He promised himself that if and when he got tired of the game, he'd sleep lightly.

Except that he hadn't. He fell asleep playing the game, barely having the presence of mind to sit the laptop aside before passing out. He slept through the power outage, and did not wake when both the laptop and the television shut off, as well as the baby monitor. He slept through the howling dogs and the terrified screams and the numerous gunshots. He slept through the explosion. He slept as his neighbors were murdered in their homes and out on the street. He slept, drooling on his pillow and snoring softly as two shadowy figures entered his home. He slept, unaware that in Artie Junior's nursery, a large, black crow had perched on the edge of his son's crib. He slept as the crow changed shape. He remained asleep as the bedroom door opened and a shadow fell across him, as well.

He didn't wake up until the baby screamed, and by then it was too late.

The last thing he saw was the figure in the room with him. The baby's screams turned to high-pitched, terrified shrieks. Artie bolted upright and flung the sheets off his legs, but before he could get out of bed, the intruder rushed to the bedside and loomed over him. The man's face was concealed in darkness. It shoved his chest with one cold hand and forced him back down on the bed. In the nursery, the baby's screams abruptly ceased.

"W-who...?"

"Scream," the shadow told Artie. "It's better when you scream."

Here is the real-life version of events:

Brian Keene slept, which was exactly what he'd been afraid of. His wife of seven years, Cassi, was out of town. She worked as a corporate trainer for a large commercial real estate company (because her husband's income was unreliable), and once a year, all of the company's employees went on a mandatory week-long retreat. This year, they were in Utah, enjoying steak dinners and attending seminars about things like team-building and synergy. Brian liked to tease Cassi about these things, but only because he was secretly jealous. He hadn't been paid by his publishers in over six months, and it bothered him that he couldn't provide for his wife or their new son.

Brian had always been a deep sleeper. His mother had once said that he could sleep through a nuclear war, and that wasn't far from the truth. Since becoming a father for the second time around, Brian's biggest fear was that the baby would wake up crying, perhaps hungry or in need of a diaper change or shaking from a nightmare, and he'd sleep through it. That's why he was grateful when Cassi was there to get up with the baby at night, and that's why he dreaded these rare times when she wasn't home.

They had a baby monitor in the house. A small camera was mounted above the baby's crib. It broadcast a signal to the monitor, which was plugged into the bedroom's television. With Cassi out of town, Brian had turned the volume on the television all the way up, filling the room with white noise and the soft sounds of his son's breathing. Then, bathed in the glow from the screen, he'd sat back in bed with his laptop and worked on a television treatment for a show that he was pretty sure would never get off the ground. The production company for a very popular sitcom actor had asked Brian to write a treatment for a post-apocalyptic zombie sitcom, and even though Brian thought that was the stupidest fucking idea he'd heard in quite some time, he did it because his family needed the money. It was early—too early to sleep, but the baby had been tired and cranky, and Brian knew from experience that he should rest when the baby rested. He promised himself that if and when he got tired of working on this stupid TV pilot, he'd sleep lightly.

Except that he hadn't. He fell asleep writing, barely having the presence of mind to set the laptop aside before passing out. He slept, drooling on his pillow and snoring softly— until voices began coming from the television speakers.

The first thing he became aware of was a burst of static. This was followed by a soft, feminine voice. The woman was speaking, forming distinct syllables and words, but he couldn't tell what they were. She paused, and his son, not quite two years old, answered her with baby talk. As he woke fully, it simultaneously occurred to Brian that a) this wasn't a dream, and b) the voice was originating from his son's bedroom.

Brian bolted upright, flung the sheets off his legs, and stared at the television screen. There was his son's room. The baby was awake, and standing up in his crib. He wasn't crying. Wasn't scared. He was babbling, as if his mother or father were in the room with him. Except that that was impossible, because his mother was in Utah and his father was watching from bed.

"Hi," the baby said. "Hi! Hi! Hi!"

The baby jumped up and down in the crib, grinning happily as he repeated it over and over. Each joyful exclamation was punctuated with a wave of his little hand.

Brian started to get out of bed when he saw something that...

Well, okay. Enough of that third person nonsense. You get the idea. That's a nice example of merging real life with fiction. Here's what happened next.

I started to get out of bed, but then I saw something on the screen that absolutely stunned me. It was an orb, about the size of a softball. It seemed to be composed of solid light, and it was hovering next to my son's crib. The baby was standing up and waving at it. The ball hung there for a moment, as if suspended from a string. Then it zipped out of the camera's eye and vanished from my sight. I knew it was still in the room, however, because the baby was still watching it. He turned his head, following its movements.

I got out of bed and ran across the house, yelling—I don't know what I was hollering. It was just nonsense-words. Panic-speak. The language of fear.

As I ran down the hall, I spotted Sam. He was sitting outside of the baby's room, unable to get through the door because of the security-gate we have placed in front of it. His back was arched and his ears and tail were flat. He wasn't barking or growling. Instead, he was whining—a fearful, pitiful sound that scared me even more. This wasn't a fucking hallucination, because the dog and the baby were all experiencing it, too.

I opened the gate and Sam pushed past me and barreled into the room. I was right behind him. The baby looked at us, smiled and then clapped his hands.

"Hi, Da-Da! Hi, Dog-Dog! Hi!"

The room was empty and dark, save for the night light glowing on the dresser. There were no orbs of light, hovering or otherwise. I shivered, and then realized that I was cold. No, it wasn't just me. It was the room. My son reached for me, and I bent over and picked him up. He snuggled up against me, lovingly, trying to burrow into my chest. Normally, that's one of the most wonderful and sweet feelings in the world, but this time, it barely registered with me. Sam nosed around the crib, sniffing furiously, his Beagle genetics working overtime to catch a scent. Holding the baby tight, I checked the little thermometer hanging above the changing table. Sam began sniffing the rest of the room. According to the thermometer, it was fifty degrees in the baby's room. That couldn't be right. I had the heater set to seventy-three throughout the house. As if to confirm this, it kicked on while I stood there staring dumbly at the wall. Warm air blew out of the floor vent, bathing my bare feet. I carried the baby (who was now wide-awake) out of the room and checked the thermostat in the living room.

The house was at seventy-three degrees.

We walked back down the hall, and I shut the door to the baby's room. Then I sat him down on the floor in the kitchen to play while I got some things together. I grabbed his diaper bag and changed his diaper there on the floor. Then I got dressed and rounded up the baby and the dog and took them both out to the car. I strapped the baby into his car seat. The dog sat next to him, tongue lolling, his ears back up, his eyes wide with excitement. Sam loves to ride in the car, but a midnight ride with the baby in tow was something new for him. I started the car and left the engine running so that it would warm up inside. I went back into the house.

When I walked through the door, I gasped. The baby's train was singing "Chugga chugga, choo choo, spin around. Every letter has a sound."

Next to it, the baby's Elmo doll was chattering in that all-too-recognizable-to-all-parents high-pitched voice, asking me for a hug. And beneath the sound of both, I heard that phantom cell phone beeping in my son's room.

"What do you want?" I shouted, staring around the living room. "What the fuck do you want from us?"

"Can you give me a hug, please?" Elmo asked.

"Chugga chugga, choo choo, spin around. Every letter has a sound."

My hands curled into fists at my sides. "You leave my fucking son alone! Do you hear me? Get the fuck out of here and leave us alone!"

Everything stopped.

Somehow, that was even more frightening.

I grabbed the cat (she was hiding beneath the coffee table

and when I picked her up, I felt her little heart hammering against my palm). Then I carried her outside, put her in the car with the dog and the baby, and we drove around for the rest of the night. The baby fell asleep. The dog and the cat rode in silence. I listened to *Coast to Coast AM* with George Noory and a Howard Stern replay and tried to keep my hands from shaking.

Near dawn, I pulled into my parents' driveway. It was their day to watch the baby, but normally, I don't bring him to their house until 8am. It wasn't even six yet. When Mom asked why we were there so early, I told her that he'd had trouble sleeping and I'd resorted to driving him around all night. It was as close to the truth as I wanted to get.

I crashed in my old room in a bed that no longer fits me, and when I woke up later, I asked my parents if they'd enjoy it if the baby and I spent the night. They said they would.

I didn't go back home until Cassi returned three days later.

ENTRY 15:

That takes us back up to the present. Or at least a close proximity of the present. After the baby monitor incident, things quieted down again. I still heard the occasional beeping sound. The baby still looked at the top of the driveway and waved hello. I still had the dreams once in a while, and Cassi was still uncomfortable smoking on the deck at night. But the glider didn't rock anymore, at least, not that I'd seen. There were no floating orbs. No "Chugga chugga, choo choo, spin around. Every letter has a sound." No Elmo asking me for a hug.

I didn't tell anyone about what happened. I didn't want

them to think I was crazy.

And here we are. When I started writing this diary, I was forty-one, and as I finish it, I've been forty-two for a few months. Other than that, not much has changed.

It is December 19, 2009 and as I type this, the Mid-Atlantic is in the midst of one mean motherfucker of a snowstorm. Earlier, I took a yardstick outside of my office and measured the accumulation. In the non-drift areas, we have twelve inches of snow. The National Weather Service is predicting we could have a lot more. I think they're right, since the snow shows no signs of abating. On Twitter, Dave Thomas (my sometimes assistant, better known to the world as Meteornotes) called this DEATH STORM 2009. I think that's a good name for it. I think it's fine and proper and has a beautiful ring to it.

But then again, I'm on a death trip.

My neighbor and I have been taking turns plowing the driveway with his snow-blower. On my last trip up to the top of the driveway, I noticed that the cross was no longer there. I know it was there yesterday, because I see it every time I go up for the mail. But some time early this morning, a snowplow hit it, along with the guardrail. There are a few little pieces of wood scattered amongst the snow drifts on the side of the road, but the rest of the cross is gone. I wonder if, when the snow melts and winter passes, will the victim's family return and put up a new memorial to remember her by? Or do they remember her in other ways? Or is her memory beginning to fade?

Yesterday, after poking around online again and coming up empty (Google can tell me the average annual rainfall for Botswana, but it can't tell me who died at the top of my driveway), I decided that it was time to get serious about this whole thing. One of the benefits of having freelanced for the *York Dispatch* in the past is that I still have access to their clippings library and archives. I once featured that archival room in a novel, *Ghost Walk*. In real life, it's pretty much like I described it in the book. There is row upon row of massive filing cabinets, filled with clippings from the paper. They are arranged by alphabetical category and span decades of history—going back all the way to the paper's inception. The really old stuff is on microfilm, rather than paper, and there's some talk of digitizing the whole collection, but that costs money and newspapers are making about as much money as mid-list horror writers these days.

I drove to the newspaper's office, which is located in downtown York City, told the girl at the door who I was, and then went downstairs to the archives. Things hadn't changed since my previous visit (I'd last been there about a year and a half ago, doing research for an aborted non-fiction book on powwow magic). A few staffers recognized me, and I exchanged pleasantries and made small talk. Then I got to work.

It took me about twenty minutes to find what I was looking for. I pulled out a file, flipped through the clippings till I found the date, and there she was.

The girl on the glider.

Staring up at me from the past.

Her family had provided the newspaper with her senior photo. In it, she was smiling. I wondered what she was thinking about when it was taken. All of those possibilities that lay ahead on the road of life? The future must have seemed wide open. Little had she known, when the picture was snapped, that the road of life detoured into an embankment at the top of my driveway just a year later, and that none of those dreams or possibilities would ever come to pass.

We go through the days thinking we have our whole lives ahead of us. We put off things until tomorrow. We spend time consumed with work and obsessed with making enough money to provide for our loved ones, but in that pursuit, we sacrifice spending time with the very people we're working to support. I spend all of my days writing. That's all I fucking do. From eight in the morning until five or six at night. Write. Write. Write. Hope someone sends a check on time. Write. Write. Write some more. And at what cost? Sure, my family have a roof over their heads, but if I found out tomorrow that these tumors are no longer benign, and I only had a week to live, would it have been worth it? Would I then contact Mike and Nate and tell them that, instead of finishing whatever stupid novel is left on my computer, they spend time playing with my son instead, because I didn't have time to finish doing that either? Would I ask them to pay more attention to my wife for me, because I'd been unable to do so?

There are things I want to do in life. I want to have hobbies again. I want to become a backyard astronomer and take up amateur photography and fish in my trout stream more often. I want to ask my kids how their day was and rub my wife's feet every night and take the dog for a long walk each and every day, rain or shine. I want to spend more time with my parents, and tell them that I appreciate them and that they are loved. I want to do all of these things, but I never do. I put them off until tomorrow, so sure that I'll get them done…eventually.

But eventually doesn't always happen. The girl on the glider had dreams, too. She had things she wanted to do. I stood there, flipping through the file. There were three articles about the accident. The first simply recounted the accident details, including statements from the State Police and the County Coroner. The second was the follow-up article that I was reading. The third was her obituary. I read them all, and got to know her. I learned about her dreams and wishes and desires. She'd put them all off for whatever reason, figuring they'd happen eventually…and then she died unexpectedly at the top of my driveway.

After I'd finished, I put the file away and left the building and came back home. The sky was overcast and gray. Death Storm 2009 was approaching. I wondered what I should do next. I couldn't very well go to her parents, could I? Just show up and knock on their door and say, "Hi, I'm Brian Keene. The guy who writes those books? I'm sorry to bother you, but your daughter has been haunting my house this past year, and I was wondering if you could ask her to stop? I think she might not know that she's dead. She seems to be trying to contact someone. Have you received any weird text messages lately?" They'd have me arrested. Or shoot me. Or both.

I decided to do a little magic. I've written enough about it that I know the basics. The most important part of magic, regardless of which discipline you're practicing, is the act of naming. Names are power. If you know something's true name, it gives you power over it.

I walked to the top of the driveway. The sun had just gone down and the road was extremely dark. There was very little traffic, on account of the impending snowstorm. I stood there, shivering, hands in my pockets, and stared at the spot where the accident had occurred. Without really knowing what I was going to say, I began to speak out loud.

"Hi. My name is Brian. Now you know my name. I know your name, too. I found it today. Your name is _____. I'm really sorry for what happened to you. I've got this theory that maybe you're feeling a little lost. Maybe a little lonely? Maybe you're not sure where your friends went? Maybe you keep texting them, but nobody is calling you back."

I paused. The wind rustled the trees.

"Did you ever watch *The X-Files*? I don't know, maybe that was before your time. Maybe your parents dug it, though. I was a big fan of the show. There was this one episode where Agent Mulder is hiding out on an Indian reservation, and one of the characters quotes an old Native American saying: 'Something lives only as long as the last person who remembers it.' I'm not sure how that applies to this situation, but I'm certain that your parents and your friends remember you."

I paused again, glancing around to make sure that no one was listening. I didn't need one of my neighbors going, "Oh, look. Keene is standing at the top of the driveway talking to imaginary people."

When I was sure we were alone, I continued.

"I think you were sent here to teach me something. I think maybe that's why you can't pass on. See, I'm an agnostic when it comes to all of this spiritual stuff. I've tried Christianity and Buddhism and every other kind of 'anity' and 'ism' but at the end of the day, I lack faith—and faith is what is required of any belief system. I want to believe that there's something after this. I want very badly to believe in an afterlife, but I haven't been able to. Until now. I don't know what you are. You might be a ghost or a spirit. You might be conscious. You might just be an echo of time—a psychic after-effect. Or maybe you're just in my head. I don't know. But I know that I now believe. So I want to thank you for that. You've shown me that a part of us—some vital part of what makes us who we truly are— lives on after our death. I don't have to rely on a literary legacy of books for people to remember me after I'm gone. I don't have to bust my ass cranking out one pulp novel after another just to ensure that I live on. Something lives only as long as the last person who remembers it. If I get my shit together and change my ways, I'll live on in the memory of my kids and my grandkids and those whose lives I've touched in some way."

I reached up and wiped a tear away. I hadn't realized I was crying until just then.

"I'm forty-two. I used to think, 'Well, I'm only in my early forties. I've still got plenty of time.' But I bet you thought that, too, right. And you were only nineteen. You were only nineteen and then suddenly, it was over before it had ever even really started."

I ran out of words. My last sentence seemed to hang there in the cold air, just like my breath was doing.

"I'm not sure what happens next. I'm going to go back down to the house and start living. Try to save my marriage. Try to be a better father. Maybe you should look around for a light or something. They say there's supposed to be one on that side. I don't know. If you can't find one, I guess you're welcome to stay here, I guess. Anyway, thanks again."

My shoulders slumped. I suddenly felt very silly. I walked

back down to the house, went out to my office, and turned off my computer. My Blackberry was flashing at me, informing me that I had voice mail and unanswered text messages. I turned it off without reading or listening to them. I stayed long enough to pat Max on the head and show him a little extra attention. Then I went inside the house.

Cassi and the baby were in the living room. The dog and cat were lying on the couch. The baby was playing with his train. He looked up, saw me, and smiled.

"Hi, Da-da!"

"Hi, buddy. How are you? What are you doing?"

"Choo-choo train. Da-da push!"

So I did. I pushed him all around the living room, and sang along with the toy as I did.

"Chugga chugga, choo choo, spin around. Every letter has a sound."

ENTRY 16:

There was over a foot of snow in the driveway this morning, and when I went outside, I saw footprints in the snow. They started at the top of the driveway, came down to our house, circled both our cars, came up onto the porch, and then went back up the driveway again.

My neighbor told me later that he saw what made them. It was a stray dog. A Husky, with a collar on. We're going to try to catch it later, and find it a home.

Just a dog. Nothing more.

No dreams last night, and no work today.

I've got more important things to do.

I'll work when I'm dead.

MUSINGS

This happened to me last night, and I need to talk about it to someone, and since my publisher is after me to get a story turned in on time, that someone is you. Call it meta-fiction if you like, except that there's not much fiction to it.

It was just before six in the evening. My girlfriend had gone home at nine that morning, and I'd been writing non-stop all day. That doesn't sound like hard work, typing words on a laptop for nine hours, and it's not, in the grand scheme of things. I've had hard jobs—sweating in a foundry, moving boxes on the loading docks, driving a tractor trailer for fifteen-hour stretches. Writing is a breeze compared to those, and a lot more fun. Still, it was a lot easier to write for nine hours straight when I was in my twenties than it is in my early forties. My back hurt, my wrists ached, and my fingers were stiff with the onset of arthritis—a relatively new affliction that biology and genetics had given me for a forty-second birthday present last year.

I decided to take a break, and while I was brewing a fresh pot of coffee, it occurred to me how quiet the house seemed, and how lonely I was. I've got my youngest son Mondays through Thursdays, and my girlfriend visits me when she can, but when the two of them aren't here, I spend my time alone and spend my alone time writing. Writing is a solitary act, and it makes for a solitary existence. Hell, I should know. Writing is the reason I'm alone. I'm good at it—writing, I mean. I'm not so good at being alone, despite the fact that it's how I spend my life. But I'm good at writing, or at least, that's what my editors and publishers tell me. I sometimes suspect they only tell me that because I make them lots of money. People will tell you whatever they think you want to hear when you're making them a lot of money. I've often wanted to purposely write a bad book, just so I can see their false praise for what it is, but I wouldn't do that to my fans and readers. And I wouldn't do it to myself. Because other than being a father, writing is the only thing I'm good at. It's the only constant in my life. The only thing I can always count on.

And all it cost me was everything else.

For starters, writing has resulted in two failed marriages. One in my twenties, when I was living in a trailer with a young wife and infant son, working all day in a factory and coming home at night to try my hand at becoming the next Joe Lansdale or David Schow or Skipp and Spector. Another in my thirties, when I'd succeeded in my career as a writer, and was living in a nice house with a wonderful second wife and another infant son, writing all day and then writing all night, as well, just to stay on top of the heap of bills and keep a roof over our heads.

Writing has also cost me friends—both from before I became a writer and after. Childhood chums, pissed off that I mined so much of our lives for fiction. Friends from high school and old Navy buddies who I no longer had anything in common with, who assumed that just because they saw my books in stores or my movies on television that I must somehow be wealthy and hey, could I lend them a few dollars or help them get published or be the dancing monkey and star attraction to impress all their friends and family members with at their next Christmas party. Fellow writers and peers, people I'd come up with, promised to do it together with, only to have them lose touch with me when I got successful.

Or maybe it was me who lost touch with them. Maybe it was my own insecurities—my own guilt at achieving everything we'd all hoped for, while they still hadn't. And maybe that applied to those old high school friends, as well. Maybe they were just proud of me, and I mistook that pride for something else. And maybe those childhood chums were right to be angry. Perhaps not all of our personal demons needed to end up as grist for my fiction mill. And maybe—just maybe—my two ex-wives had been right to expect me to choose a healthy relationship with them instead of fifteen hours at a keyboard living inside my own head seven days a week, instead of talking to them or living with them.

Those were the thoughts that kept me awake some nights, and on those nights, I drank more whiskey and continued to write. It was a self-perpetuating vicious cycle. Lose everything because of writing until the only thing you have left is the writing itself. Rinse and repeat.

But it's too late to do anything about it now. And like I said, I'm good at it. So I have that going for me. And not everything has been lost. I have great relationships with both of my sons. My youngest is four, and even though his mother couldn't be married to a writer any longer, we remain best friends and work well together as co-parents. My oldest is twenty-one, and although he's a young man now, when I look at him I still see the little boy who read through his daddy's comic book collection and played superheroes on my living room floor for hours and talked about how he was going to be a writer just like me when he grew up. Thank God and Cthulhu he didn't. That desire lasted exactly one season when he was ten. Now he's a senior at Penn State and studying to be a social worker. The pride and love I feel for him is as tangible as the lump I get in my throat when I think about how much he's grown. He doesn't talk about writing anymore, and for that I am grateful. I only hope that his younger brother does the same. My oldest son doesn't read my books and his only association with them is when he goes to science fiction, fantasy, and horror conventions wearing a t-shirt with one of my book covers on it. When a cute girl approaches him and compliments the shirt and tells him they are a fan of my work, he smiles and says, "Yeah, he's my dad." I'm okay with this. I will probably never leave either of my sons a lofty inheritance, so the very least I can do is get them laid.

My relationship with my girlfriend is good, too. Maybe that's because we're both writers. We know exactly what goes into this life of ours, and what the demands are. But I suspect that same knowledge is what keeps us from permanently cementing this relationship and making it official. Because we know that no matter how close we are, we'll always have a laptop between us—or two laptops, in our case. Because we know that sooner or later, the good things will go away, leaving only fodder for the muse.

Because that's how the muse gets fed.

In U2's "The Fly," Bono sings that every poet is a cannibal and every artist is a thief. They all kill their inspiration and then sing about the grief. Until last Saturday night, I believed this to be true.

I know better now.

It's not the artist who kills their inspiration.

It's the inspiration that kills the artist.

* * *

The coffee had finished brewing but my brain and body were still sore. Worse, loneliness and isolation were still weighing on me. I could have reached out to someone. I could have called my girlfriend, or any of the other people I truly trust—a group whose members sadly dwindle with each passing year. But doing so would have alleviated my melancholy, and I needed that melancholy to write. Yeah, talk about job security. "Continue to feel bad so you'll write better."

So instead of reaching out and touching someone, I decided to extend my break and go for a walk. I live in a remote section of rural South-Central Pennsylvania, down in the bottoms of the Susquehanna River, an area so backwoods that it makes the rest of the county look positively metropolitan in comparison. I like it that way. I like seeing greenery and wildlife outside my window. I like having no traffic zipping by all day or noisy neighbors or sidewalks or a convenience store or bar within walking—or even driving—distance.

I put on my jacket and grabbed my walking stick—a sturdy length of oak that had originally belonged to my grandfather, faded now and worn smooth by his hands and mine. I miss my grandfather. He passed several years ago. Using that stick always makes me think of him. Worse, it always makes me wonder if he was ever proud of what I'd accomplished as a writer or if, like the rest of my family, he quietly (and sometimes openly in the case of a few family members) wished I'd give up this writing thing and get a proper job again. Something else I missed when I went for a walk was my dog. Writing had cost me him, too, in a way—lost in that second, amicable divorce. Oh, I still saw him on an almost daily basis, and he was always happy to see me, wagging his tail and grinning that dog grin that hounds do so well. But it wasn't the same. Gone were the days when I'd write for fifteen hours with him lying at my feet, patiently waiting for me to finish so we could go for a walk and decompress before rejoining the rest of the world, already in progress. These days, he lives with my second ex-wife, and her boyfriend is the one taking him for walks, and I write alone.

I walk alone, too.

I pulled a cigar from my humidor, clipped it, lit it, and headed out the door, clutching the walking stick and feeling the weight of my thoughts. I'm not supposed to smoke cigars anymore, especially after my heart attack. Wrath James White, F. Paul Wilson, and Joe Lansdale have all threatened to kick my ass if I continue, so if you read this, don't tell them I was. It will be our little secret.

Anyway, I walked down to the river. The weather suited my mood. It was that weird time of day—not quite nightfall but not the end of daylight, either. The overcast sky was colored with muted shades of gray and white, and a persistent breeze rustled the leaves on the trees, knocking them to the ground in a cascade of reds, oranges, and yellows. Nice weather for hunters, Goths, moody horror writers, and malcontents, but other folks probably prefer spring or summer. The river was deserted. When it's warmer outside, the waterway is packed with boats—blue-collar guys out fishing in aluminum bass boats, rich yuppies up from Maryland for the day in their obscene pleasure boats, and thrill-seekers on Jet Skis. The river banks were usually packed, as well, with family picnics and folks feeding the ducks. But they'd all gone home for the season, and the ducks had flown south, and on the day they'd left, I'd wished I could go with them.

There was one lone car in the parking area—a blue Mazda with a Penn State bumper sticker on the back, and some additional stickers for bands I had never heard of, because I am in my forties now and stopped listening to new music right around the time that hip-hop got turned into hit-pop and Kurt Cobain did us the disservice of killing heavy metal before killing himself. Far away, down near the chain link fence that sealed off the gravel service road for the Safe Harbor Dam, I saw three college-aged girls, and assumed the car belonged to them. They were too far away to notice anything else about them, so I turned my attention back to the river. I stood there, hands in pockets, smoking and thinking, and gearing myself up to go back home and write some more. As I watched, the sun slipped beneath the horizon, and blue gave way to black.

I stood there until my cigar was finished. Then I tossed the stub into the water and turned to leave. As I did, I noticed the three girls approaching. They were close enough now that I was able to get a better look at them, and what I saw left me stunned. I don't know if it was the fact that I'm now middle-aged or the loneliness I'd been feeling prior, but I absolutely could not take my gaze away from them. They appeared to be twenty, maybe twenty-one. The first was blonde with blue eyes. The second had dark hair and even darker skin. The third girl was a brunette. Their nationalities were hard to pin. I saw hints of Caucasian, African, Asian, Indian, and more—an exotic mix of genetics and heredity that suggested the entire world had been distilled into these three beauties. They reminded me of pop princesses—or barely legal porn starlets—and at that moment, I felt very old and very ashamed, and I'm not sure why.

I nodded hello and turned away, determined not to be the creepy middle-aged guy I felt like, when the blonde disarmed me with a smile and a question.

"Working on a new book?"

I'm used to getting recognized, especially near my home. No, I never had to deal with the level of notoriety Stephen King did after filming that credit card commercial, but I've got enough of an Internet presence that I'm easily identifiable. It's a given this happens at conventions or signings, but I've also encountered it occasionally in airports, the grocery store, at movie theatres, and once in a bathroom at an Amtrak station. And as I said, it happens fairly regularly in my hometown (local boy made good, and all that). So it wasn't the girl's question that threw me, nor was it the fact that she apparently knew who I was. What left me flummoxed was the sensation that I knew these girls from somewhere. I'd never signed a book for them. Of that, I was certain. I'm good with faces, and if you've stood in line to get my signature, chances are I'll remember your face, if not your name. I was certain that our paths hadn't crossed in that way, but the instant connection I felt with them was so strong that it left me feeling nervous and dizzy.

All three stood there staring at me, smiling, and I realized that I hadn't responded.

"Taking a break from one, actually." I tried to smile, but it probably looked like I was having a seizure. Whatever my expression, it was apparently amusing, because all three giggled softly. Their laughter was like music. I felt my body begin to thrum.

What the hell is wrong with me? I thought. I felt like a character out of one of my books. You know the one where the Satyr comes back to life and everyone is running around with a hard-on? It was like that, except that this was real life, and the sensations coursing through me weren't just sexual. Don't get me wrong. Lust—or maybe longing—was a definite component. But it was something more than that. It was...*need.* On a primal, spiritual level. I didn't understand it, but that didn't stop me from feeling it. Even though I didn't know why, I felt that I needed these women.

We made small talk for a while. The girls had a slight, almost unrecognizable accent that I couldn't place. I don't remember everything that was said. I started out with my public patter, accessing the stores of anecdotes and witty responses I keep for any occasion when I'm talking with fans, but soon enough, I found myself relaxing, and becoming the real me. The girls must have noticed this, too. They didn't tell me their names, and I didn't think to ask, so flustered and confused was I, puzzling over my own behavior. I remember asking if they went to school around here, thinking they had to be from Penn State or York College. It turned out they didn't, although they had plans to visit the Penn State campus the next day. When I told them my son was enrolled there, they smiled again. When I asked why they were planning to visit the campus, the brunette told me they were from Boeotia, and were just traveling. I'd never heard of Boeotia, but didn't mention it because I didn't want to seem rude. When I asked what brought them to the river bottoms of York County, they told me I had. They were fans, and they'd known I lived nearby, and they'd wanted to see me.

We talked a while longer, and when the moon and the stars finally peeked out from behind the cloud cover, the temperature dropped. Shivering inside my leather jacket, I told them I had to be getting home. They offered me a ride back, and I accepted. I'm still not sure why. I'm not one to let the public know the exact whereabouts of my home. I use a PO Box and don't allow friends to post pictures taken outside my home on Facebook. Hell, I'm so concerned with privacy, that I don't even mention either of my son's names in public. And yet, quite uncharacteristically, I was allowing these three girls to give me a lift back to my front door.

And when we got there, I let them come inside.

One trip to my liquor cabinet later, and the booze, conversation, and laughter were flowing freely. They admired my bookshelves, which made me happy. They exclaimed over first edition Peter Straub books and rare volumes by M.R. James and Edward Lee. My signed copy of Arthur Machen's *Strange Roads* elicited a smile from all three, and when I asked them if they were familiar with his work, the brunette said, "Oh, yes. We knew him." I was buzzed enough that I let the odd response slip by, assuming she meant they knew of his work, even in far-off Boeotia. They'd probably read *The Great God Pan* in high school or something. The girls seemed particularly interested in my books by Hunter S. Thompson, Robert E. Howard, Karl Edward Wagner, Ernest Hemingway, Edward Lucas White, Edgar Allan Poe, and other writers who'd had notoriously rough lives and even rougher endings. The three seemed well-versed and knowledgeable in their works—something that amazed me at the time. It's not often you meet three college-aged beauties with whom you can discuss what makes Wagner's "Sticks" the most effective horror short story ever, or the stark, fearful sub-text of Thompson's post-9/11 "Where Were You When the Fun Stopped?"

I was well into my second bottle of bourbon and the girls were working their way through my tequila, having finished off the last of my Sambuca (a gift from my girlfriend), when we ended up collapsing onto the bed together. Looking back, I had no misgivings about this. It never occurred to me that it was inappropriate. It seemed like the most natural thing in the world. I felt safe. Secure. That feeling continued as I poured my heart out to them, telling them things the rest of the world didn't know, things I've never even told my friends, truths about myself that have only been told as lies in my fiction. And I was still feeling safe and secure when they retrieved four of my ties from the closet and secured my wrists and ankles to the bedposts. Then they went to work on me with lips and tongues and fingertips, and only once did I resist—a half-hearted protest that dissipated almost before leaving my mouth.

As they swarmed over me, soft hair grazing my skin,

raising goose bumps with its passage, they whispered and murmured the truth to me. They told me how my writing was for shit these days, and how I needed to experience pain once again. They spoke of how my best works, the books for which I'm known, stemmed from turmoil and heartache—the death of a loved one, the dissolution of a marriage, the loss of a child, struggles with substance abuse and depression. Those things fed and informed my fiction, and I needed to return to those things once again. They teased that I'd grown fat and old and bald and content, and my current output was a reflection of that. I needed to be hungry again. I needed to hurt again.

Their words changed, as did their faces. It felt like I was viewing them from the end of a long, spiraling tunnel. I passed out with their bodies as blankets, and the voices ceased.

When I woke today, my head was numb and my mouth tasted like the inside of a gorilla's stomach. My first sensation, before even opening my eyes, was an overwhelming sense of guilt. I'd cheated on my girlfriend. I'd callously betrayed her trust for a drunken tryst that I couldn't even remember clearly. Just what had happened anyway? The ties were gone and my limbs were free. I remembered skin and hair and softness. Security. Had I cried at some point? I think I had, but couldn't remember why.

Glancing at the clock, I was stunned to see that it was late evening. I'd nearly slept the entire day. I sat up, groaning at the stiffness in my limbs. The girls weren't in the bedroom, and the house was quiet, so I assumed they were gone.

I was partially right.

I stumbled downstairs to make some coffee, and found my laptop open on the dining room table. The screen glowed softly. My cell phone lay next to it. I picked up the phone first, checking to see if I'd missed any calls or texts, and was alarmed to see several texts sent to my girlfriend from my phone sometime after I'd passed out. I clicked on the texts and groaned. Somebody had taken pictures of me and my visitors, and judging by the fact that each picture showed me and two of the girls, but a different combo in each shot, it had to have been them. Worse, they'd then texted these pictures to my girlfriend—who was either still asleep and hadn't gotten them yet, or was so distraught that she hadn't even been capable of responding.

Panicked, I collapsed into a chair and reached for my laptop. I had some vague, terror-driven notion of Googling a way to delete texts that had already been sent, but before I could do that, I saw an open Word document on my screen. It repeated what they'd whispered the night before, of how I needed to hurt again, and of the new works that would spring forth from that pain. The note was signed with love from Melete, Mneme, and Aoide.

I knew those names. They were the names of the three Muses worshipped in ancient times on Mount Helicon in…

…in Boeotia.

"Fuck you!"

The words fell flat in my empty kitchen. I'd meant to shout them, but all I managed to do was croak. I sat there, crying and cursing and pounding my fist against the table. All three gestures were ineffective. Then, stomach churning, I dashed for the bathroom, barely making it in time before the sourness of the previous night's libations ended up in the toilet. I knelt there, gasping and sweating and puking some more, and almost passed out again. I heard my phone ringing, but was in no condition to answer it. Eventually, when the tremors had subsided, I crawled to the sink, pulled myself upright, and splashed water on my face. I stared into the mirror and cringed at what I saw staring back at me.

My phone dinged, alerting me that I had a voice mail. I returned to the kitchen and reached for the phone with trepidation, expecting it to be my girlfriend. Instead, it was my oldest son. I held the phone to my ear and listened to his message. It sounded like he was calling me from a frat party, judging by the noise in the background. Amidst the white noise, I heard lilting female laughter—and almost screamed at the sound.

"You'll never guess what happened to me," my son was saying. "I'm at this party on campus and I met these three girls. They're fans of your work. I'm heading back to my place with them now. They're totally fucking hot. I'm turning my phone off so we don't get interrupted. You know what I mean. Anyway, just wanted to say thanks, Dad!"

I called him back, but got no answer. I called both of my ex-wives but there was no answer from them, either. Nor my girlfriend. Nor my family members.

I was alone again. Truly alone. Just me and my laptop.

It occurred to me that I should call the police, both locally and on campus. Have them check on the status of my loved ones. Make sure they were safe. Give them a description of the three women. I'd have to be careful not to sound like a madman. I couldn't very well say that these women were serial killers. That they murdered for their host's inspiration, killing everything good in the artist's life until there was nothing left. That they might be going by the aliases of Melete, Mneme, and Aoide, but that they had other aliases, as well, like Nete, Mese, and Hypate, or Cephisso, Apollonis, and Borysthenis. They'd lock me up if I said these women had killed Poe and Thompson and Hemingway and so many others. No. Instead I'd just tell the authorities that these were three disturbed fans of my work, and that I had strong reason to believe that my loved ones were in danger.

And that's what I intended to do.

But it was important that I write this first.

I'll make those calls soon.

I just need to write another thousand words or so before I do. I haven't been this productive in a while...

GOLDEN BOY

I shit gold.

It started around the time I hit puberty. I thought there was something wrong with me. Cancer or parasites or something like that, because when I looked down into the bowl, a golden turd was sitting on the bottom. When I wiped, there were gold stains on the toilet paper. Then I flushed and went back to watching cartoons. Ten minutes later, I'd forgotten all about it.

You know how kids are.

But it wasn't just my shit. I pissed gold. (No golden showers jokes, please. I've heard them all before.) I started sweating gold. It oozed out of my pores in droplets, drying on my skin in flakes. It peeled off easily enough. Just like dead skin after a bad case of sunburn. Then my spit and mucous started turning into gold. I'd hock gold nuggets onto the sidewalk. One day, I was picking mulberries from a tree in a pasture. There was a barbed-wire fence beneath the tree, and to reach the higher branches, I stood on the fence. I lost my balance and the barbed-wire took three big chunks out of the back of my thigh. My blood was liquid gold. And like I said, this was around puberty, so you can only imagine what my wet dreams were like. Many nights, instead of waking up wet and sticky, I woke up with a hard, metallic mess on my sheets and in my pajamas.

Understand, my bodily fluids weren't just gold-colored. If they had been, things might have turned out differently. But they were actual gold—that precious metal coveted all over the world. Gold—the source of wars and peace, the rise of empires and their eventual collapse, murders and robberies, wealth and poverty, love and hate.

My parents figured it out soon enough. So did the first doctor they took me to. Oh, yeah. That doctor was very interested. He wanted to keep me for observation. Wanted to conduct some more tests. He said all this with his doctor voice but you could see the greed in his eyes.

And he was just the first.

Mom and Dad weren't having any of that. They took me home and told me this was going to be our little secret. I was special. I had a gift from God. A wonderful, magnificent talent—but one that might be misunderstood by others. They wanted to help me avoid that, they said. Didn't want me to be made fun of or taken advantage of. Even now, I honestly think they meant it at the time. They believed that their intentions were for the best. But you know what they say about good intentions. The road to hell is paved with them. That's bullshit, of course.

The road to hell is paved with fucking gold.

My parents started skimming my residue. Mom scraped gold dust from my clothes and the sheets when she did laundry and from the rim of my glass after dinner. One night, they told me I couldn't watch my favorite TV show because I wouldn't eat my broccoli. I cried gold tears. After that, it seemed like they made me cry a lot.

Everywhere I went, I left a trail of gold behind me. My parents collected it, invested it, and soon, we moved to a bigger house in a nicer neighborhood with a better school. Our family of three grew. We had a maid and a cook and groundskeepers.

I hated it, at first. The new house was too big. We'd been a blue-collar family. Now, Mom and Dad didn't work anymore and I suddenly found myself thrown into classrooms with a bunch of snobby rich kids—all because of my gift. I had nothing in common with my classmates. They talked about books and music that I'd never heard of, and argued politics and civic responsibilities and French Impressionism. They idolized Che Guevara and Ayn Rand and Ernest Hemingway. I read comic books and listened to hip-hop and liked Spider-Man.

So I tried to fit in. Nobody wants to be hated. It's human nature—wanting to be liked by your peers. Soon enough, I found a way. I let them in on my little secret. Within a week, I was the most popular kid in school. I had more friends than I knew what to do with. Everybody wanted to be friends with the golden boy. But here's the thing. They didn't want to be friends with me because of who I was. They wanted to be friends with me because of *who* I was. There's a big difference between those two things.

So I had friends. Girlfriends, too.

I remember the first girl I ever loved. She was beautiful. There's nothing as powerful or pure or unstable as first love. I thought about her constantly. Stared at her in class. Dreamed of her at night. And when she returned my interest, my body felt like a coiled spring. It was the happiest day of my life. But she didn't love me for who I was. Like everyone else, she loved me for *who* I was.

So have all the rest. Both ex-wives and the string of long-term girlfriends between them. My happiest relationships are one-night stands. The only women I'm truly comfortable with are the ones I only know for a few brief hours. I never tell them who I am or what I can do. And before you ask, yes, I always wear a condom and no, I can't have children. There are no little golden boys in my future. I don't shoot blanks. I shoot bullets.

I've no shortage of job opportunities. Banks, financial groups, precious metals dealers, jewelers, even several governments. Of course, I don't need to work. I can live off my talent for the rest of my life. So can everyone else around me. But that doesn't stop the employment offers from coming. And they're so insincere and patronizing. So very fucking patronizing. They want to invest in my future. Just like my parents and my friends and my wives, they only want what's best for me. Or so they claim.

But I know what they really want.

And I can't take it anymore.

I'm spent. My gold is tarnished. It's lost its gleam. Its shine. I can see it, and I wonder if others are noticing, too.

Here's what's going to happen. I'm going to put this gun to my head and blow my brains out all over the room, leaving a golden spray pattern on the wall. The medical examiner will pick skull fragments and gold nuggets out of the plaster. The mortician can line his pockets before embalming me. You can sell my remains on eBay, and invest in them, and fight over what's left.

I want to fade away, but gold never fades. This is my gift. This is my legacy. This is my curse.

I have only one thing to leave behind.

You can spend me when I'm gone.

THE ELEVENTH MUSE

Every Sunday afternoon, Roy eats lunch at the Great American. He waits until after the church crowd have all gone home to watch whatever sporting event is on TV, because the restaurant is much quieter without them. Roy likes to people watch. He's a writer. People watching is part of his job description. But he also likes to be able to enjoy his meal without a constant barrage of sound from the other tables.

Roy walks in the door, waits a minute, and is then shown to a booth by the hostess. He sits facing the door, pleased to note that there are only a handful of other diners—an elderly couple who are very obviously still in love, a young couple just as obviously on a first date, a single father with his pre-teen daughter, and a family of four skirting the edge of divorce. Roy determines these things with a few quick glances, using the deductive skills employed by mental health professionals, fictional detectives, and writers like himself.

Unlike many people their age, the elderly couple still have things to say to each other, rather than sitting in silence. More importantly, there is still contact between the two, be it their eyes or the touch of fingertip to the back of the other's hand.

There is no touching between the young couple, although

there is a lot of furtive eye contact. The air between them is absolutely brimming with nervous energy. Roy can hear it in their forced laughter, and their even more-forced attempts at small talk.

It is easy to see the genetic resemblance between the father and daughter. He wears no wedding ring, and desperately tries to make conversation with the girl, who is more interested in the conversation she's having with someone else via text. She gives him short, clipped, one-word answers, saving the multi-syllable responses for whomever is on the other end of her phone. The man seems sad, and he also keeps checking his watch, seeing how much time they have left together.

And the family of four aren't talking. Or rather, the kids are talking, but the mother and father don't talk to each other. The children's expressions are sad and pensive. The mother's expression is grim. The father's eye keeps wandering to the woman on the first date.

The other reason Roy waits to come to the restaurant until after the crowds have dispersed is because being around all those people makes him feel lonely. Unfortunately, delaying his arrival hasn't helped today. He wants to go over to the elderly couple and tell them how envious he is of them and offer to pay for their meal. He wants to do the same for the young people on their first date. He wants to remind the divorced dad that he still has someone in his life, and he should be happy for that. And he wants to jerk the father of two out of his booth and smack some sense into him. He wants to remind each of them that it can all end at any second—that the world is nothing more than a monster that feeds on goodness and kindness and love, and that the beast grows hungrier by the day.

Roy doesn't do any of these things. Instead, he pulls out his Kindle, turns it on, and picks up where he last left off. Today's book is David Schow's *Havoc Swims Jaded*. There's a chance he may finish it before finishing his meal. If so, he'll switch over to the latest by Greg Rucka or Weston Ochse. Roy usually reads four or five books a week, depending on his own deadlines. He's never been much for television, and his DVD collection takes up only one single shelf. He prefers to read, and since he spends so much of his life alone, he has plenty of time for that.

He has plenty of time for writing, too, although for the last year, that has been a problem.

Roy has writer's block, which is ironic since for most of his career, he has insisted that this malady doesn't exist— that it is nothing more than an excuse lazy writers invent for not getting work done. But now, after twenty years and thirty books, Roy finds himself unable to write. He still goes through the motions every day. He sits down at his laptop and opens up a document file and types a few words, but that's as far as he ever gets. He used to average five thousand words a day. Now he averages five. Roy finds himself distracted by trips to the coffee pot and trips to the bathroom; by social media and games and all the other things his phone contains; by music and the squirrels outside his window; by the words of other writers that line his bookshelves and the conversations of his neighbors half-heard through the thin walls of his apartment.

But mostly, Roy is distracted by the loud silence in his head.

He doesn't know where the silence comes from, but he wishes it would go away and be replaced with something else.

An idea. A line of dialogue that sounds real. A clever turn of phrase. Anything. He used to write novels that made readers feel things. Now, it's all just empty words. He doesn't feel anything, so how can he make his readers feel anything in return.

Roy saw a therapist twice—which was the maximum amount of visits he could afford. The therapist told him he was suffering from chronic depression, but Roy disagrees with this diagnosis. If he had depression, he'd feel depressed. That's the problem. Roy doesn't feel anything. He is only… numb.

He is trying not to think about this and focus instead on his Kindle, and doesn't realize the waitress is standing beside him until she clears her throat.

"Sorry," Roy apologizes.

"It's okay." The waitress smiles.

Roy is immediately struck by her beauty. She has one of those faces and bodies that appear perpetually young. She could be in her twenties or thirties. She has dark hair, dark eyes, and dark complexion. Her accent is exotic but hard to place. Eastern Europe, perhaps? He can't be sure. The only thing he is certain of is that she is new. Roy eats here every week, and he has never seen her before. She wears the same uniform as the rest of the wait-staff—green shirt and black slacks—but even those look new. He notices she has no nametag clipped to her shirt.

She nods at the Kindle. "Are you reading one of yours or someone else's?"

"Oh…someone else's. I'm guessing one of your co-workers told you I was a writer?"

She shakes her head.

Roy is surprised. "You've read my stuff?"

WHERE WE LIVE AND DIE

"I've read everything you've written. Or, at least, I used to. Although it's been a while. You're not working on anything new."

Roy notices that she phrases this as an assumption, rather than a question. It leaves him feeling flustered and a little defensive.

"Oh, I am. It's just…going slow. Writer's block."

"I thought there was no such thing."

"Whomever told you that was a liar."

"Aren't all writers liars? Especially fiction writers?"

"No." Roy clears his throat, his exasperation growing stronger.

The waitress laughs, and Roy swears there is a melody in that sound.

"Relax, Roy. I'm just teasing. Of course writers aren't liars. Especially fiction writers. They tell the truths nobody wants to hear. The truths everyone feels inside, but don't have the courage or ability to voice out loud."

"That's very astute. I take it you want to be a writer, as well?"

"No. I love art—writing, music, painting—art in all its forms. But I'm happy just to inspire."

Now Roy smiles. "You would have made a fine muse back in the day. You would have fit right in with Calliope, Clio, Erato, and the other six."

"Seven," the waitress corrects him.

Roy frowns. "I thought there were nine muses?"

"There were. But then Plato named Sappho the tenth muse."

"Huh." Roy shrugs. "Learn something new every day."

"Benefits of a classical education."

111

"What college did you go to?"

She shrugs. "Several different ones."

Roy wonders if that means she dropped out or if she pursued different degrees. Before he can ask, the waitress glances back at the kitchen, and then down at Roy. She puts her pen to pad and begins to write.

"Porterhouse, rare, with garlic mashed potatoes on the side and an unsweetened iced tea, no lemon?"

Roy is genuinely surprised. "Wow. How did you…how did you know that?"

The reflection of fluorescent lights overhead flicker in her eyes. "It's what you always order. I'll be right back with some rolls."

She glides off with a toss of her hair, leaving Roy to sit there bemused and perplexed. He assumes that one of their other staff members must have told her what he orders, because it's true—he orders the same thing almost every week, occasionally breaking it up with a taco salad or the fish and chips. It's an easy explanation. What isn't so easily explained is the almost instant connection he feels toward her. It's not sexual. Not exactly. Yes, there's a component of that, but it's not lost on him that she's half his age and far out of his league. No, this attraction runs deeper than that. The waitress reminds Roy of someone from his past, but when he thinks about it, he is unsure who. He can't help but feel that he has known her before.

Ultimately, Roy ascribes it to loneliness. A friendly, pretty, intelligent girl made conversation with him. Of course he felt something. And wonderful that was—to feel again, if only for a moment.

A different waitress walks by, attending to the other

patrons. Roy recognizes her. She has waited on him before. Her nametag says she is MARSHA. She smiles and nods at him as she walks by. Roy returns the gesture.

Yes, he decides, *Marsha must have told the new girl. I bet she also told her how well I tip.*

He does, always leaving at least twenty-five percent. Roy is aware that a lot of people in this small town know who he is, even if they'd rather chew broken glass than read a book for pleasure. He is also aware that they assume all writers must be as financially well-off as Stephen King, Nora Roberts, and John Grisham. Roy is not. He mostly lives royalty check to royalty check, and those are beginning to dry up, due to his prolonged period of inactivity. Despite his encroaching poverty, he always tips well, worried that his fellow townspeople will see him as a cheapskate if he doesn't. It's the same reason he's polite to store clerks and always gives the right of way when driving. Appearances are important, especially in a small town.

He's thinking about this when his waitress returns with his iced tea and some dinner rolls. She sets them down in front of him.

"Thanks," Roy says.

"You're welcome."

"So, if you don't mind me asking, how did you end up working here?"

"My previous employer laid me off."

"I'm sorry. There's a lot of that going around these days."

"I'm sorry, too. But this job isn't so bad. It's something to do until I find another. And it's good for people watching."

"You're a people watcher too, huh?"

"Oh, yes. I like living vicariously."

Roy grins. "Yeah, I do a fair amount of that."

"I know."

Roy blinks. "You do?"

The waitress nods. "I know that you're lonely. I know you feel trapped in a job with no 401K, no retirement, and no health insurance. I know that job feels more pointless every day, and you keep wondering what the point is."

"Trust me, a lot of writers in my pay range feel that way."

"I know that your last girlfriend moved out a year and a half ago. You met her at a book signing. She was a fan of your work. Before she moved out, she told you that while the fantasy of dating you had been exciting, the reality of being in a relationship with you was anything but. You did not blame her. You've never liked living with yourself either. I know that when you were writing, you spent all day in your head. I know that you're doing that still, but now your head is empty. I know that your parents are dead, you have no siblings, and no children, and no heirs. For the last year, you've been wondering who to will your literary estate to, and it bothers you that there's no one to assign the rights to your work. I know that—"

"Wait a second," Roy says, louder than he intended. "This is getting creepy. What did you do, Google me back there in the kitchen? Don't believe everything you read about me online."

"I know that the reason you can't write anymore is because you don't have anything left to feel. You don't remember what it's like to love someone, or hate someone, or to fear them or want to keep them safe. You're numb, and how could you not be, when looking at the world around you? A writer's job is to study the world and the people around them and mirror it back to the reader—to unveil truths. But the truth is, Roy, you don't know what the truth is anymore. When you look at the world, all you see is loss and regret and heartache. All you feel is loneliness. You don't understand the world anymore, and you no longer feel like you're a part of it. You've watched others for so long that you no longer know how to relate to them. And when you look around, all you see is horror. Everything is cancer and terrorism, and humanity's increasing descent into regressive post-modern barbarism. Your numbness grows every time you turn on the news. Every missing child, every massacre, and every bureaucratic injustice makes you disconnect a little bit more. And so, you push away anyone who was close to you or matters to you, and try to take comfort in strangers and people on the internet—because you can keep them at arm's length, and therefore they won't hurt or disappoint you. You push away your muse, your lovers, and your friends, until you're left with nothing to write about except the horror of everyday life."

Roy wants to make a joke. He wants to tell her that maybe she should switch over to writing garishly-covered horror novels instead, but when he opens his mouth to speak, all that escapes is a low sigh.

"No offense, Roy, but do your job. If hopelessness and betrayal and terror are all you know now, then let yourself feel them. More importantly, let your world feel them. You're an artist. Make art. The laptop screen is your canvas. If that doesn't work, then try a new form of canvas. But it's time for you to start telling the truth again."

Roy nods, still unable to speak. The waitress gives him a sad smile and then walks away.

He sits there, head hung low, staring at the table. He doesn't look up again until Marsha brings him his meal. It occurs to him to ask about the other waitress but he still doesn't trust himself to speak.

He eats slowly, considering what she's said. Marsha brings him his check, which he pays, leaving a thirty percent tip. Then he leaves, and heads back to his car.

A few minutes later, Roy opens the door to his apartment. He sees the couch and the coffee table that his girlfriend left behind. He sees the worn, brown carpet that was new decades ago when this apartment complex was built. The kitchen appliances and bathroom fixtures are just as dated. The blinds over the windows are new, but only because Roy bought them himself when he first moved in. Everything else in the apartment is either broken or failing. The windows are drafty, the water pressure sucks, the bathroom mirror is cracked, the molding around the front door is loose, and the heating takes forever to warm the place. The chipped paint on the walls is a dingy shade of cream, and is about twelve coats thick. If you look closely at the walls you can see hair and dirt embedded in the previous layers of paint, and poorly patched nail holes left over from previous tenants.

Before today's lunch, the decrepitude deepened his depression. Now, it inspires him.

Roy scans the living room, looking at his possessions. A plasma television which is only four years old and already shows ghost images in the upper right hand corner. A DVD player that was new back when most people still bought videotapes. A few framed photographs of people he no longer feels anything for. And books. Six cheap pressboard bookshelves bought at Walmart and put together over a long, frustrating weekend, crammed with over two-thousand paperbacks, hardcovers, first editions, and signed limited edition collectibles.

In the bedroom, there are six more shelves, also stuffed with books, but these are all ones that have been written by Roy, along with magazines, anthologies, and other outlets that have featured his work. The bedroom also has a cheap pressboard desk (purchased the same weekend he bought the shelves). His laptop and printer occupy the desk, along with stacks of miscellaneous papers receipts and dirty coffee cups. The laptop is on its last leg. It takes forever to start, and the battery only lasts a few minutes when it's not plugged in, and the question mark key doesn't work. Anytime Roy wants to type a question mark into a manuscript he's working on, he has to open Google, find an image of a question mark, and then copy and paste it into the document. Luckily, due to the writer's block, he hasn't used the laptop much in the past year. The bedroom also has a bed, and next to that, a rifle cabinet, containing the various firearms he used when he was still an avid hunter. He hasn't gone much in the last five years. As he gets older, the cold bothers Roy more and more. But he still has all the guns.

Roy realizes that the only things of value that he owns are the books and the firearms. Everything else is shit. The police will probably take the guns as evidence later, but what of the books? They'll probably be unceremoniously tossed in the dumpsters by the apartment complex management. He's seen this happen before, almost on a weekly basis. Someone doesn't pay rent, the sheriff puts a notice on their apartment door, and they abscond in the night, leaving behind their belongings, which management then tosses in the dumpsters. He's seen furniture, bedding, toys, and even electronics equipment thrown away in such a manner, and has also seen his neighbors dumpster diving for it all after management has left. He thinks about his books filling up a dumpster, and the illiterate tenants picking through them, looking for DVDs or videogames because who the hell reads anymore? For a brief moment, this image is almost enough to make Roy reconsider his decision.

But then, shrugging, he walks into the bedroom, opens his rifle cabinet, and takes out an AR-15 rifle and a .357 handgun.

Nobody reads anymore.

His muse was right. He needs to reflect and communicate the horrors of the world around him.

The restaurant will be his first new canvas and he will paint it red.

As he drives toward it, Roy hopes the other patrons will still be there.

THE HOUSE
OF USHERS

"What's the worst thing you've ever done?"

Michaels didn't answer. He, Adam, and Terrell were hunkered down in an alley behind a stack of corpses. Raw sewage bubbled up from the cracked pavement, soaking their knees and feet with filth. The black sky boiled and spit. Instead of hail, decapitated heads fell from the clouds. Michaels hoped the storm would end soon. He much preferred rains of blood or shit—they didn't hurt when they struck you.

Terrell tapped Adam on the shoulder.

"What?" Adam whispered.

"Check this out."

Terrell buried his face between the rotting breasts of a particularly obese corpse and made motorboat sounds. The mounds of flesh jiggled, disturbing a nest of beetles that had burrowed inside them. Terrell came up for air and picked insects and decaying flesh from his chin. He and Adam giggled.

Ignoring them, Michaels peeked over the carrion pile and stared at the barracks. Nothing had changed. Two Ushers still stood out front, guarding the door. Their chisel-slit eyes remained alert, and their nostrils flared. They did not move. Shivering, Michaels ducked down again and glared at Adam.

"What did you ask me?"

Adam repeated it. "What's the worst thing you've ever done?"

"The worst thing I ever did was let you assholes talk me into doing this."

Terrell grinned. It was not a flattering look for him. Every day, the Mephistopolis blossomed with new diseases, and Terrell always caught them. It had been the same way when he was alive. Any time a new venereal disease came along, Terrell got it. As above, so below. This week, the flesh was sloughing off his face in waxy, glistening sheets.

"Come on, Michaels," he slurred. "You want out of here as bad as we do. So don't even front."

"Of course I do. But there's got to be a better way."

Even as he said it, Michaels knew it wasn't true. This was the only way, unless they wanted to wait for another Deadpass to open somewhere else. Who knew how long that could take? A week, a decade, an eternity? Of course, here in Hell, every day was an eternity. Terrified as he was, Michaels knew this was their only shot at escaping— right through the very bowels of Hell—into the House of Ushers. Deadpasses—holes between the living world and the Hellplanes—were few and far between. The only other ways out were through the Labyrinth, ascendancy to demon-hood, or divine intervention. As slim as the chances were of finding another Deadpass, those options were even less viable. Adam's plan was their only opportunity to escape.

A head splattered against the pavement, showering them with brains and interrupting Michaels's thoughts.

"Seriously," Adam asked a third time. "What's the worst

thing you've ever done? Humor me."

Michaels sighed. "First of all, you're ripping off Peter Straub. That's the opening sentence to *Ghost Story*. You're a writer. That's theft—a sin."

Adam shrugged. "Have you taken a look around? Given our current situation, I don't think that matters. It's one small sin among a sea of great ones. The end result is the same. And you're right. It is the opening sentence to *Ghost Story*. But it's a good sentence. It has presence and weight. It fucking resonates, man. If you hit it with a hammer, you'd hear a resounding gong. So I'm stealing it."

Michaels grinned. "Is that the worst thing you've ever done?"

"No..."

Adam fell silent, suddenly afraid. Each man felt it. In Hell, the obsidian sky never changed. There were no moons or sun. Daylight was a memory from their previous existence. But now, against that churning blackness, a shadow soared overhead—predatory and horrifying. For something to inspire fear in this place, it had to be exceptional, and the shadow was. It glided over the city, blotting out the falling heads.

A dead cat hissed at the far end of the alley. The cat had seen better days. Apparently, it had been mummified at some point during its existence. Dirty, tattered bandages hung from its skeletal frame. Without warning, the shadow swept down from the sky. It made no sound as it attacked. Something black and shapeless seized the howling cat and the shadow took flight again, leaving coldness in its wake.

All three men shivered.

"Yo," Terrell whispered, "we can't keep hiding behind

this pile of dead bodies. If that thing—whatever it was—don't get us, then the damn garbage trolls will."

"He's right," Michaels said. "They'll be along to load these corpses into a Meat Truck any time now."

Terrell nodded. "We need to get the fuck inside those barracks."

"Not yet," Adam cautioned. "We can't do shit until they send a squad out. If we go in there before the Ushers leave, we'll be outnumbered—toast."

Three more heads exploded across the pavement. Michaels wished for an umbrella.

"We're going to be toast anyway," he said. "So why don't you fucking answer your own question while we wait, Adam? What's the worst thing *you've* ever done?"

Adam paused. When he spoke again, they had to strain to hear him over the constant wails of the damned. His eyes were wet and red.

"I killed my wife. She was pregnant. The kid...wasn't mine. I lost my mind. Made it look like an accident, pushed her out of the attic window. That's what got me here."

"Jesus Christ..."

Terrell flinched. "Michaels! You know you ain't supposed to say that name here. The fuck is wrong with you? Want to lead them right to us? You'll bring all of Hell down on us."

"Sorry."

Adam wiped away his tears. "How about you guys? What did you do to wind up here?"

"I shot a baby," Terrell said. "My crew was at the zoo, tracking down this bitch that ripped us off. Found her with this baby. Boss-man told me to shoot the baby. I hesitated, but you know how it is. Peer pressure and shit. If I hadn't done it, that would have been it for my ass. So I did. And then the bitch we were chasing shot me and I woke up here."

Michaels shook his head, disgusted and speechless.

"What?" Terrell glared at him. "You too good to be here, Michaels? You an innocent man? You here by mistake?"

"I don't *know* why I'm here," Michaels said, "but it's certainly not because I killed somebody. I just lived my life. I'm not an evil person."

Adam started to respond, but a wailing siren cut him off. All three men risked another peek at the Usher barracks. Red lights flashed inside as the alarm continued to blare. Sulfurous smoke belched from the tall, crooked chimney on top of the building. In the alley, the pavement rumbled beneath their feet.

Michaels gasped. "Feel that?"

"Fuck," Terrell whispered, "it's a stampede."

"It's not a stampede," Adam said. "It's our chance. Cross your fingers."

Frightened, Terrell grabbed Michaels's hand and squeezed. Michaels returned the gesture. Terrell's ulcerated skin burst, squirting pus between Michaels's fingers, but Michaels didn't mind. In truth, he barely noticed. His attention was focused on the House of Ushers. Even though he didn't need to anymore, he forgot to breathe.

Adam leaned forward, watching intently. "Here we go. They're sending out a squad. Soon as they leave, the barracks will be empty—just a few Ushers and a skeleton crew. All we have to do is make it past them, find the basement, and go through the Deadpass. Then we're home free."

Michaels rolled his eyes. "Oh, yeah, no problem—easy as pie."

"Do you want to back out? Because now is the time."

"No. But these are fucking Ushers, Adam. They fuck and they kill and they fuck what they kill. That's what they're bred for—pain and mutilation and rape. It's like trying to kill a bull with a toothpick."

Adam shook his head. "They're not invincible."

"Shit," Terrell said, "they're damn close. Can't kill the fuckers on Earth."

"No, we can't," Adam agreed, "but we *can* kill them here. Ushers can die in Hell. Blow their heads off, chop them up, cut out their hearts—and the benevolent damned can cast spells on them here, too."

"Except," Michaels reminded him, "none of us are benevolent damned."

"No," Adam said, "we aren't. But we do have weapons. And they'll work."

"They better," Terrell said. "I had to suck the pus out of a thousand infected clits just to score these things."

"You'd have done that anyway."

"Fuck you, Adam. I didn't like eating pussy when I was alive, and I sure as shit don't like it now."

Ignoring him, Adam lifted the legs of a corpse and pulled out a large sack. He'd stashed it beneath the bodies when they arrived, safeguarding it from discovery in case they were captured. He opened the sack and reached inside. Michaels and Terrell crowded around him. The first thing Adam pulled out was a sword. The blade was long and thin and very sharp—forged in the Mephistopolis. The metal held a reddish tint, and glinted in the firelight. The hilt was fashioned to depict a mockery of the crucifixion; Christ hung upside down, nailed through the eyes as well as the wrists and feet, his face leering with a madman's grin, his penis replaced with a crude gaping vagina. Michaels shuddered as he accepted the weapon from Adam. It felt unclean.

Adam produced a second weapon from the sack; a pistol, remarkably similar to a Wilson Combat 1911, but it was manufactured from the black bones of a Great Wyrm. The magazine held ghoul talons instead of bullets. The deadly projectiles had hollow centers, and each one contained a corrosive, acidic center. Terrell held the pistol sideways, so that the sights were pointing to the left.

"That's what I'm talking about." He nodded in satisfaction.

"You're holding it wrong," Michaels told him.

"That's how they do it in the movies."

"Fire it like that and the acid's gonna splash back on you."

"Shit." Terrell sneered, and more of his face fell off. "Ain't no brass flying out of this thing. Acid gonna go out the front. And besides, you see my motherfucking skin? Acid burns would be an improvement on that shit."

Michaels shrugged. "Suit yourself."

Adam pulled out a collapsible shotgun, the twin-barrels folded over the stock. He snapped it into place and locked the hinge with a cotter pin carved from the fang of a Vamphyr. Then he reached into his coat pocket and smiled.

"What kind of ammo does that thing take?" Terrell asked.

Still smiling, Adam pulled his hand from his pocket and opened his fingers. Rough lumps of melted silver lay in his palm. Michaels and Terrell both gasped in surprise. Adam dropped the loads down both barrels.

"Yo," Terrell asked, "where the fuck did you get silver?"

"You don't want to know. Let's just say I paid a price and leave it at that."

Michaels studied the weapon. "How's it going to fire? Don't you need some kind of primer or powder?"

"Nope," Adam said. "Trust me, it'll work just fine. Remember that angel they captured last month? Before it died, I snuck into the dungeons and had the angel bless the shotgun. It shoots spells, and never runs out of ammo. The silver is just an extra measure."

Michaels whistled with appreciation. "You thought ahead."

"That's right," Adam said. "Every step of the way. Soon as I found out there was a Deadpass inside the House of Ushers' basement, I started planning. So relax. I'm telling you, this will work."

"It better."

"What you got back on Earth, anyway?" Terrell asked. "What's so important, Michaels?"

"You mean escaping from Hell isn't reason enough?"

"For me and Adam, sure. But you're different. Could be you don't belong here, like you say. But whether you do or don't, I ain't never met a man that wanted out of here more than you do. I can tell. I read people like books."

"Is that so?" Michaels raised his middle finger. "Here. Can you read sign language?"

The barracks' doors flew open and an Usher battalion poured out into the street. Adam, Terrell, and Michaels hugged the pavement, biting their lips and praying to the God who'd condemned them here that they wouldn't be spotted. The Ushers were dressed for urban riot control—studded leather armor with blood-stained, razor-sharp spikes and edges; great, curved weapons with sigils etched into the blades; firearms that could disintegrate a body with one fiery blast; massive clubs that could pulp the heads of a dozen men with one blow. But the armament was more for psychological use than practical. The Ushers didn't even need it. Their inhuman design was one of Hell's most enduring and efficient legacies. An Usher's claws could rend steel and their jaws and teeth were powerful enough to chew through bedrock. They would lay waste at random, decimating a city block and slaying all who dwelled there. They would rape, dismember, torture, and kill—then do it all over again to anything that was left, regardless of whether it was still recognizable or even intact, all in the name of civil obedience and of keeping the populace on its toes.

All to retain the status quo.

Trembling, Michaels dared to peek over the corpses and watched the battalion march out of sight. The Ushers moved like a column of ants. There were hundreds of them and their stench was terrible. Cloven feet pounded the pavement. The buildings swayed from the vibration. The damned stopped wailing, terrified into silence.

Michaels didn't notice that both Adam and Terrell had pissed themselves because he was too busy doing the same.

After the column had marched out of sight, the three men stood up. Still concealed in the alley, they peered out at the House of Ushers. The barracks were silent. The two guards were still positioned at the door, but their attention was focused farther down the street, where a baby vendor was serving up roasted infants on hot buns and loading them with ketchup, mustard, onions and relish. The vendor handed the treats to three minor demons, who greedily devoured them. Watching, the Ushers drooled, but did not leave their post.

"They're distracted." Adam readied the shotgun, holding

it slightly upright so the silver wouldn't slip out of the barrels. "You guys ready?"

"Let's do this shit," Terrell said.

Michaels gripped the sword and nodded. He was too afraid to speak.

Adam strode out of the alley and quickly crossed the street. After a moment's hesitation, Michaels and Terrell followed. As they drew closer, one of the Ushers turned toward them, broad nostrils flaring, catching their scent. It grunted, more out of annoyance than surprise. Snorting, it took a single step in their direction. The pavement grew black where it trod. Adam faltered. Behind him, Michaels and Terrell prepared to run.

Then Adam shot the Usher in the face.

The shotgun belched greenish-white flame. The creature reared backward, clawing at its eyes. Crackling energy clung to its head. Its mottled flesh sizzled, sloughing off in sheets. Michaels sniffed the air. Above the stench of sulfur and shit and his own piss, he smelled cooked meat. His stomach grumbled. He hadn't eaten in a year.

Bellowing, the wounded Usher collapsed to its knees, and then tottered forward, dead. Its flesh continued to bubble and fizz. The other guard rushed toward them. It made no sound, but its eyes said all they needed to know. Michaels raised his sword with trembling hands and braced himself for the charge. He shut his eyes and whimpered. Adam's shotgun rang out again. Michaels heard the second Usher fall. He opened his eyes and stared in disbelief. Both creatures had been dispatched.

"Holy shit."

"Indeed," Adam said. "Now let's keep moving."

They dashed up the steps and halted in front of the closed door. This close to the barracks, the building's aura nauseated them. Michaels fought to keep from puking. He didn't need to, of course. There was nothing in his stomach *to* puke up. But the old habits of living died hard.

"What the fuck we waiting for?" Terrell reached for the handle.

"Don't," Adam warned him, but it was too late.

Terrell's hand wrapped around the door handle. Immediately, the brass twisted, coming to life. Metallic tendrils coiled around his fingers and squeezed. His bones snapped. Terrell screamed. The tendrils climbed higher, racing up his wrist and forearm, pulling him closer.

"The sword," Adam yelled. "Michaels, cut him loose."

"I can't just—"

"Do it, motherfucker," Terrell shrieked. His eyes rolled into the back of his head and his teeth chattered with pain and shock. "It ain't like the shit ain't gonna grow back again. Cut it off, man!"

Michaels raised the sword, hesitating.

Adam shoved him. "What are you waiting for?"

Terrell moaned. The coils had reached his elbow. More bones snapped. Blood flowed. Cursing, Michaels brought the sword down, cleaving Terrell's arm just above the elbow. The hilt grew warm in his hands, and the carved figure of Christ sighed against his palm. Disgusted, Michaels almost dropped the sword.

Terrell stared at his stump. Blood jetted from the wound. The tentacles crushed the severed appendage into paste.

Then they slowly reformed into a doorknob.

"I'm sorry, man," Michaels apologized. "There wasn't anything else we could do."

Terrell grinned. "Shit, it don't matter. Like I said, it'll grow back. They always do in this place. Long as I can still hold this pistol, it ain't no thing."

He demonstrated, posing like Wesley Snipes in *New Jack City*.

"You're still holding it wrong," Michaels told him. "You're gonna fuck yourself up."

Terrell nodded at his stump. "Can't be no worse than this."

"We're wasting time," Adam said, glancing down the deserted street. "The head storm's over. No telling when the street will get busy again."

"Well," Terrell said, his voice indignant. "Let's see you open the fucking thing."

Nodding, Adam stepped closer to the door. Then he whispered in a language the others had never heard. When he was finished, he stepped backward. Slowly, the door creaked open. The stench that wafted out was revolting—a charnel miasma that seemed to cling to them.

Michaels gaped. "Where did you learn to do that?"

"Same place I got the weapons. The language is Sumerian."

"But what did it mean? Those words you said?"

"I don't know. It's the Ushers' password. Probably something nasty."

"We gonna stand here all night?" Terrell asked. "Thought you said time's a wasting."

Adam swept his arm out and bowed. "Lead the way."

"Shit. Don't look at me."

"Then get out of the way." Adam pushed past Terrell and entered the House of Ushers. Michaels crept along behind him. Terrell hesitated, and then followed.

They passed through a foyer carved from black marble and stepped into a large room, obviously bigger inside than the barracks' outside dimensions. The high, vaulted ceilings stretched hundreds of feet over their heads, and the walls were barely visible on the horizon. Endless rows of bunk beds ran the length of the room, stacked three high. The frames were constructed from stone and the pillows and mattresses were stuffed with human hair. Blonde locks spilled from a torn pillow. The mattresses and pillowcases were made out of human skin.

"My God," Michaels gasped. His voice echoed in the vast chamber.

God...God...God...

"Dude!" Adam punched his shoulder in anger. "Don't fucking say that name here. They'll be on us quicker than you can blink."

"Sorry. It's just...so big. It's kind of hard to wrap my brain around, you know?"

Adam nodded. "It's bigger on the inside than it is on the outside—some kind of interspatial dimension thing."

"Are you sure all the Ushers are gone? Can this place really be deserted?"

"No. Like I said before, there's still the skeleton crew to deal with. That's why we need to keep moving. Find the Deadpass before they find us."

"True that," Terrell said. His stump had stopped bleeding. "Let's get the fuck out of here."

"We're going home," Michaels whispered, trying to convince himself that it was true.

"According to my sources," Adam said, pointing to their left, "the basement stairs should be over that way."

Michaels balked. "How far?"

"About a quarter of a mile."

"My Go..."

Adam and Terrell tensed, but Michaels stopped himself from finishing the word in time.

"Sorry."

They walked on, side by side, weapons at the ready. Their footsteps rang out. Otherwise, the barracks were silent. They passed by what looked like a bath of some kind—a stone circle surrounding a depression in the floor. Words and figures were carved in the masonry, but none of them could read it. The pool was filled with black, stagnant liquid.

"What's that?" Michaels whispered.

Adam shook his head. "I don't know. An Usher foot bath, maybe?"

"I'm serious."

"So am I. I don't know what it is, but that water looks pretty nasty."

Terrell reached into his pocket and pulled out a coin. Hitler's face was engraved on one side. Reverend Jim Baker's face decorated the other.

"What are you doing?" Adam asked.

"Making a wish."

Balancing the coin on the ball of his thumb, Terrell flicked it into the pool. It made no sound as it broke the surface, but small concentric rings spread out across the water, lapping at the stones. Then the rings began to run backwards, drawing into the center of the pool. As they watched, the liquid began to congeal. A small pseudo-pod formed in the middle of the water and then rose into the air, growing in size.

"I got a bad feeling about this," Terrell moaned.

"Move!" Adam shoved them both forward.

They ran past the bath. Behind them, the black tentacle waved about in the air like a snake. Then it collapsed back into the pool.

Adam glared at Terrell. "Quit fucking around."

"Yo, how was I supposed to know that shit was alive?"

Michaels glanced back the way they'd come. "What was that thing, anyway?"

"I don't know," Adam said. "Something bad, obviously. There's nothing good in here. All the more reason for us to get out. Now, let's keep moving, and for fuck's sake, Terrell, don't touch anything else."

They moved on, searching for the basement stairs, trying to ignore the horrors around them. Obscene tapestries and paintings adorned the walls. One of them depicted the Virgin Mary in a bukkake scene with the twelve disciples. Another showed the prophet Mohammed receiving anal from a particularly well-endowed demon. A third was of the Whore of Babylon riding astride a multi-headed beast. Each of the creature's faces was that of a world leader. American Presidents, British Prime Ministers, and military despots leered down at them. The tip of the beast's penis—which was small in comparison to the rest of its size—also had a face.

Gawking, Michaels pointed. "Isn't that Bush?"

"Sure is." Adam grinned. "Always knew he was a dickhead." All three of them laughed. The sound echoed throughout the barracks, and they fell silent again. Then they continued on their way.

"Do you guys really want to know the worst thing I've ever done?" Michaels asked.

They nodded.

"I was married. My wife, Linda, was my world. I loved her like you wouldn't believe. You ever love somebody so much that your stomach hurts?"

"Yeah," Adam whispered. "I have."

"Well, that was how I felt about Linda. But I ignored her. Not on purpose. I bought her nice things. Gave her security—a nice home, nice car. But I didn't pay attention to her needs. I worked for an online brokerage. Long hours. Climbing the corporate ladder. Same old story. I focused on my career. Dedicated myself to achieving my goals— becoming what I'd always wanted to be. I was following my dreams, and I expected Linda to follow them with me. She was my wife, after all. She should support me."

"Damn straight," Terrell said. "Bitches ain't shit but hoes and tricks."

"Shut up," Michaels grumbled. "It's not like that at all. Linda had dreams, too. She wanted to have kids. That's all. Just two kids—a boy and a girl. But I kept putting it off. Told her I needed to focus on my career. And then, five years later, Linda got ovarian cancer."

Adam paused. "Shit."

"Yeah," Michaels said, leading them forward. "She survived, but the doctors said she'd never be able to have kids. If we'd started trying earlier—if I hadn't made her wait. But I ignored her desires. That's why I'm here."

"That ain't so bad," Terrell said. "You must have done worse shit than that."

Michaels shook his head. "No. That's my greatest sin. She's getting married again. Next week, in fact. The demons have been taunting me with it, torturing me by showing me scenes of her new life. She looks happy."

"Sorry," Adam said. "That must be tough to watch."

Michaels shrugged. "I pretend it is. I scream and wail and do everything the demons expect me to do. But the truth is, I'm happy for her. Seeing Linda like that and knowing that she's happy makes Hell a little more bearable. She's got a second chance, you know? Maybe Linda and her new husband can adopt. Maybe he'll pay more attention to her."

Adam stared at him in comprehension. "You're going to the wedding, aren't you? That's why you want out of here."

"Yeah," Michaels admitted. "That's my plan. I want to see her happy. Want to say I'm sorry. I never got the chance before."

"Maybe you will," Adam said.

"God, I hope so."

God...God...God...

"Damn it, Michaels!" Adam glanced around, alarmed.

A dry rasping sound echoed across the chamber.

"The fuck is that?" Terrell aimed the pistol at nothing.

"Oh shit," Adam moaned. "It's the skeleton crew."

The rasping sounds drew closer. Michaels spotted movement from several different areas, all closing in on their location. As the figures drew closer, he heard clicking, like wooden wind chimes. Then the creatures emerged into the light.

They were skeletons, bare of flesh or clothing—just white bones, polished till they gleamed. Their eyes were black holes, devoid of light. They carried an assortment of weapons—swords, maces, guns, axes, and knives. Spying the three intruders, the skeletons charged. They did not speak or shout. The only sound was the clatter of their bodies. They moved in creaking spasms.

"Fuck this." Still holding the handgun to one side, Terrell opened fire. He squeezed the trigger three times. The corrosive bullets tore into the skeletons, shattering their bones. At the same time, the ghoul talon jackets sprang from the side of the pistol—directly into Terrell's disease-ravaged face. Flinching, he dropped the pistol and screamed. Welts appeared on his flesh. They turned from red to black. His skin split open and began to bubble. Tendrils of smoke curled from his face. The welts grew wider, revealing bone and gristle. Then the acid began eating its way through that, as well.

"It burns," he screamed. "Oh motherfucker, it's eating my fucking skin off!"

His cries turned into gurgles as the acid dissolved his tongue. Terrell fell to the floor, thrashing in agony. His melted flesh spread out in a steaming pool.

The skeletons drew closer. Adam's shotgun rang out, firing spells at point blank range. Michaels swung the sword, cleaving through bones like they were butter. When an opening appeared, Adam grabbed Michaels's arm and pulled him along.

"Come on!"

They ran, almost slipping in Terrell's liquefied remains. There was nothing they could do for him. It would be at least a full day before he reformed. Dodging the skeletons, they fled down an aisle of bunks.

"The staircase!" Adam pointed. "I see it over there."

Michaels didn't respond. His lungs felt like bursting. His head throbbed.

They dashed down the black marble stairs, ignoring the carved-bone handrail, and emerged into the basement. The Deadpass glowed in the center, crackling with eldritch energies. Although it made no noise, they heard it humming inside their heads.

"That's it," Adam shouted. "We're home free, Michaels."

He ran toward the portal. Michaels followed him, but slid to a halt as a huge, dark form lumbered out from behind a vat of eyeballs and blocked their path. It was an Usher—the biggest Michaels had ever seen. Its eyes were as large as dinner plates. When it breathed, Michaels cringed. It was like standing next to a blast furnace filled with feces. The creature wore a necklace of human skulls and a loincloth made from human skin.

Adam didn't even have time to scream.

The Usher's massive hands shot out and seized him by the neck. It picked him up and turned him around. Adam's feet dangled above the floor. The shotgun fell from his hands. Grunting, the Usher turned him around. Then, still holding him aloft with one hand, it ran a talon along his backside, slicing his pants open.

Quivering, Adam pleaded with Michaels to help him. Instead, Michaels stepped backward. He heard the skeletons at the top of the stairs.

The Usher's penis sprang forward, swaying and bobbing like a snake. The thick, slimy organ pulsated in the dim light, covered with warts and sores. The Usher laughed. The sound was like sandpaper.

Moving carefully. Michaels crept around them. Adam reached for him, but Michaels looked away.

The Usher positioned its throbbing cock and pulled Adam closer.

"Michaels! Help me you bastard!"

"I'm sorry, Adam. I've got a wedding to attend. Got to get to the church on time."

The last thing Michaels heard before he leapt through the Deadpass was the condemned man's screams. Michaels considered praying for Adam, but he knew from experience that prayers for the damned were an exercise in futility.

He abandoned his friend and didn't look back.

It was the second worst thing he'd ever done.

THE REVOLUTION HAPPENED WHILE YOU WERE SLEEPING

SLEEPING

(A SUMMONING SPELL) —REMIXED

Primitive man gathers in a cave. Outside, the ice draws closer, the cold bites with teeth sharper than any carnivore. For comfort against the darkness, man invents the first story. It is a horror story.

The darkness is beautiful and filled with wonders.

Fast forward.

Beowulf, Macbeth, and Faust sing The Rime of the Ancient Mariner. The Apparition of Mrs. Veal appears to Arthur Mervyn in The Castle of Otranto. The gothic era is born when The Monk and Melmoth the Wanderer tell the Children of the Abbey the History of the Caliph Vathek. Dracula and Frankenstein; or, the Modern Prometheus as his friends call him, investigate The Strange Case of Doctor Jekyll and Mr. Hyde at Wuthering Heights while The Sorcerer's Apprentice reads The Diary of a Madman.

The darkness grows stronger.

The Pit and the Pendulum swings, ushering in a new era, A Descent into the Maelstrom. The Black Cat and The Gold Bug play Hop-Frog over The Cask of Amontillado during The Fall of the House of Usher. Childe Roland to the Dark Tower Came, and upon his arrival, used The Monkey's Paw to activate The Turn of the Screw.

The Death of Halpin Frayser occurs in The House of the Seven Gables, directly beneath The Yellow Sign. The King in Yellow flees on The Phantom Rickshaw, while The Purple Cloud follows in his wake. The Great God Pan watches as The Ghost Pirates escape on The Boats of the Glen Carrig, and sail into The Night Land. Count Magnus spies The Picture of Dorian Gray in A Shop in Go-By Street.

The Call of Cthulhu echoes over The House On The Borderland At The Mountains of Madness. The Wendigo stalks The Dead Valley, where Lukundoo administers The Mark of the Beast at The Camp of the Dog, while listening to The Music of Erich Zann.

The Shadow Over Innsmouth grows longer. The darkness grows stronger.

The Fury of the third age brings Dangerous Visions and Dark Forces. The Doll That Ate Its Mother is a Psycho. He shouts I Am Legend and I Have No Mouth And I Must Scream. The Exorcist chases Rosemary's Baby and All Heads Turn When The Hunt Goes By. The Manitou sits in The Dark of Charnel House, listening to The Rats. Christine and Carrie open The Books of Blood and tell a Ghost Story. Tread Softly on this Dark Mountain, for The Watchers with the Twilight Eyes are there, playing The Damnation Game, causing Misery to the Lost Souls while the Hot Blood runs and runs again over The Bridge. The Breeder does the Goat Dance to the beat of The Tommyknockers and The Kill Riff.

Then The Cleanup begins. The AfterAge. The Swan Song. The darkness is swallowed by a garish day-glo. Its lifeblood is drained dry by one too many vampires run amok.

The darkness goes away.

This is where we come in. Think of us as EMT's. We check the pulse of the genre, and though it is dead, we fight to bring it back.

Subterranean by design, we dance the Cemetery Dance at our Leisure. In Delirium, we tell DarkTales of the Eraserhead. We throw down the Gauntlet, slide down the Razor Blade, and in the Night Shade we eat our Flesh & Blood Medium Rare. It's Prime time.

Now is the time of Natural Selection. The time of Maternal Instinct. We are the Deadliest of the Species and we stand firm. The Distance Travelled was a long one, but there is No Rest For The Wicked. We see in Colors. Broken in our Sorrow, we cry Salt Water Tears. We are the Dregs of Society—Deadfellas—the Holy Rollers. As The Sun Goes Down we gather an army of Scary Rednecks and Other Inbred Horrors that reek of Bum Piss and Other City Scents. Partners In Chyme, we prepare a feast of Shoggoth Cacciatore and drink The Blood of A Blackbird. The Spectres and Darkness celebrate This Symbiotic Fascination. Ghosts, Spirits, Computers and World Machines deliver The Big Punch, while Dead Cats Bounce.

Wake up!

We came of age while the genre was Among The Missing. We crawled from The Cellar of the Beast House during the Off Season. We were the Lot Lizards; Incubi and Succubi taking in the Nightlife and celebrating Ladies Night while we stared Deep Into That Darkness, Peering at The Light At The End of the Road To Hell. You did not hear us coming because the din of your dark echo rang in your ears. This is your wake up call. The revolution happened while you were sleeping…

And the darkness has never been stronger.

THINGS THEY DON'T TEACH YOU IN WRITING CLASS

BRIAN KEENE'S HELPFUL WRITING TIPS THAT NO ONE ELSE WILL TEACH YOU

1. Never say, "Well, life can't get any worse." Because that is when life will invariably kick you in the teeth.

2. In the end, the only people you can really trust are your kids. All others are suspect, even your cat or dog.

3. Yes, your kids can break your heart, too, but that takes years. Your dog or cat will eat your face after just a week with no food.

4. Except for maybe the Six-Million Dollar Man's bionic dog. But the dog on the original *Battlestar Galactica*? That dog would have totally eaten Boxey's face.

5. They say that success breeds contempt, but they are misinformed. Success breeds one thing—loneliness.

6. Before you are successful, you have friends. Once you

are successful, you have more friends. You will also attract sycophants.

7. Some sycophants don't mean to be sycophants. Others do. It can be very hard to tell a sycophant from a friend. They are like John Carpenter's *The Thing*.

8. Worse, some friends can become sycophants. Even your pre-success friends are not immune to this transformation. So you adopt an attitude of "Trust No One."

9. The problem with that is you can no longer tell the difference. So you end up treating your friends like sycophants and your sycophants like friends.

10. And after that, you build a wall, just like in the Pink Floyd song. Eventually, you either go insane, become an addict, kill yourself, or push back and clean fucking house.

11. If you love your kids, as I do, the first three ain't an option. So you choose number four. And after you've cleaned house, you find yourself truly alone for the first time in a very long time.

12. Success breeds loneliness, but it is in that loneliness that you can finally breathe and hear yourself think, and in that silence, truly start to live.

Notes About Writing About Writing

THE GIRL ON THE GLIDER

This was originally published as a limited edition hardcover from Cemetery Dance Publications. It also appeared in my collection *A Conspiracy of One* (which is out of print) and my collection *All Dark, All The Time*. I think it fair to say that this is my twist on the traditional ghost story—a meta-fictional mash-up of M.R. James and Hunter S. Thompson. Although I don't usually care for my work after I've finished writing it, I'm proud of this one. I honestly think it's one of the best things I've ever written. But it's also the saddest. I wrote this as a last ditch effort to save my troubled marriage—a marriage that had been mostly good up until the pressures of writing for a living began to impact it. Those pressures, slow to build but oh-so-fucking-heavy, are detailed here.

Since its initial publication, people have often asked me which parts of *The Girl on the Glider* were true, and which parts were fiction. Honestly, ninety-nine point nine percent of this was true. All of the behind-the-scenes angst and drama and fuckery that was going on—I didn't make that shit up. That's exactly what it's like to make your living as a mid-list horror novelist. There is no 401K. There is no health insurance. And publishers never pay you on time. The other stuff was true, too—everything from Coop fishing a dead body out of the river to the image I saw on my son's baby monitor. A girl really did die at the top of my driveway, and she really did teach me an important lesson.

Sadly, the lesson came too late. I said above that ninety-nine point nine percent of this story was true. The part I made up...the part that was fiction? Well, that was the happy ending. In real life, the story didn't end so well. I finished writing this novella in December of 2009. Three weeks later, in January of 2010, my wife of eight years, a woman who I'd been with for sixteen years, asked me for a separation...and eventually a divorce. And she was right to do so. She was absolutely right to do so. The lessons that the girl on the glider taught me came too late. I didn't realize that then, but I do now. At the time, I blamed everyone around us. But the blame lay elsewhere...

Several years have passed, and my ex-wife and I remain best friends. Indeed, I think we get along better now than we ever did during those past sixteen years. We've both grown a lot. So has our son. Our son is healthy and happy and has two parents who love him. And I still don't blame her. Not one bit. Nobody should have to live with the guy in this novella, the guy who is chained to such an unforgiving and unhealthy job, but can't do anything else. A guy who is trapped by his muse, trapped by who he is, trapped by what he is...a guy who will never escape those things. A guy who is a writer.

MUSINGS

I used to live in a mountaintop cabin along the banks of the Susquehanna River. At the time, Cemetery Dance asked me if I'd like to be in a four-author anthology with Peter Straub, Joe R. Lansdale, and Ray Garton. That's like asking Justin Bieber if he'd like to record an album with The Beatles, Led Zeppelin, and Guns N' Roses. "Of course I want to be in that anthology," I said, and then asked about the guidelines. The only stipulation was that all the stories had to be about killers.

I thought about it for a long time. I wanted to deliver my very best for this project. At the time, *The Girl on the Glider* was getting rave reviews, so I thought maybe I should try the meta-fiction route again. I also had an idea of some of the themes I'd like to explore—how we artists seemingly sacrifice it all for our muse. As Bono sings, "Every artist is a cannibal, every poet is a thief. All kill their inspiration and sing about their grief."

While all that was swirling around in my head, I took a walk down to the river (just like in the story) and saw three girls, and everything clicked into place. I hurried back up the hill and wrote this story that night.

GOLDEN BOY

The first and last sentences of this story came to me one day, and I liked them so much that I wrote a story to tie them together. Author Kelli Owen read this story prior to its publication, and said it was a metaphor for my current place in the horror genre. At the time, I didn't believe her, but looking back on it now, she was correct. It was written at a point in my career when I could have sold my grocery list and publishers would have lined up to buy it. Thus, while at first glance, it might not seem like the story is about writing, it really is.

THE ELEVENTH MUSE

This one was inspired by my favorite waitress at a restaurant I go to every Sunday (much like the restaurant in the story and the main character's weekly ritual). I wrote it for my old friend Michael T. Huyck, who was editing an anniversary edition of *Carpe Noctem* magazine (a magazine I'd been trying to get into for almost twenty years, and finally succeeded in doing so, with this tale).

THE HOUSE OF USHERS

Back in 2009, I was asked to write a story for an Edward Lee tribute anthology. The stories all had to center around Lee's fictional version of Hell, best known from his novels *City Infernal*, *House Infernal*, and *Infernal Angel*, as well as several short stories and his wonderful collection *The Ushers* (which remains one of my top five favorite short story collections of all time). So, this story is set in that universe. If you've never read any of those, here's what you need to know about Lee's version of Hell: it's even more evil and diabolical and hopeless than the version you probably know.

You might be wondering about this story's inclusion in a collection of stories about writing. At first glance, the only relevant bit is the conversation the characters have about Peter Straub's *Ghost Story*. Here's why I included it here—the character of Adam is familiar to anyone who's read my novels *Dark Hollow* and *Ghost Walk*. He's a writer, and much of his story (especially in *Dark Hollow*) was informed by that. He is killed in *Ghost Walk* by a sentient darkness known as Nodens. This story is about what happened to him after he died.

Even in the afterlife, writers can't seem to catch a break.

THE REVOLUTION HAPPENED WHILE YOU WERE SLEEPING (A SUMMONING SPELL) - REMIXED

This is a slight reworking of a beat poem I wrote and recorded back in 2002. It first appeared on a "Brian Keene in concert" compact disc called *Talking Smack*. I think it works better when experienced audibly rather than read, but I'm including it here because it is, in fact, about writing. Its conceit is a brief history of the horror genre, and the arrival of a then-new generation of writers who would go on to become the forefront of Bizarro, Extreme Horror, New Weird, and New Pulp. I'm not going to explain it any further than that. Suffice to say, some of you will get it.

Others won't. Those that don't have my apologies, but hey, you got some other cool stories in this book, right?

THINGS THEY DON'T TEACH YOU
IN WRITING CLASS

Yeah, it's non-fiction. I included it here because I think it makes a nice thematic bookend to the stories preceding it.

BRIAN KEENE writes novels, comic books, short fiction, and occasional journalism for money. He is the author of over forty books, mostly in the horror, crime, and dark fantasy genres. Keene's novels have been translated into German, Spanish, Polish, Italian, French, Taiwanese, and many more. In addition to his own original work, Keene has written for media properties such as *Doctor Who*, *Hellboy*, *Masters of the Universe*, and *Superman*.

Several of Keene's novels have been developed for film, including *Ghoul*, *The Ties That Bind*, and *Fast Zombies Suck*. Several more are in-development or under option. Keene also serves as Executive Producer for the independent film studio Drunken Tentacle Productions. Keene also oversees Maelstrom, his own small press publishing imprint specializing in collectible limited editions, via Thunderstorm Books.

Keene's work has been praised in such diverse places as *The New York Times*, The History Channel, *The Howard Stern Show*, CNN.com, *Publishers Weekly*, Media Bistro, *Fangoria Magazine*, and *Rue Morgue*. He has won numerous awards and honors, including two Bram Stoker Awards, and a recognition from Whiteman A.F.B. (home of the B-2 Stealth Bomber) for his outreach to U.S. troops serving both overseas and abroad. A prolific public speaker, Keene has delivered talks at conventions, college campuses, theaters, and inside Central Intelligence Agency headquarters in Langley, VA.

The father of two sons, Keene lives in rural Pennsylvania.